HOW NOT TO DIVORCE A BILLIONAIRE

JULIETTE HYLAND

ROMANCE

Recycling programs for this product may not exist in your area.

ISBN-13: 978-1-335-47089-8

How Not to Divorce a Billionaire

This is a work of fiction. Names, characters, places and incidents are either the product of the author's imagination or are used fictitiously. Any resemblance to actual persons, living or dead, businesses, companies, events or locales is entirely coincidental.

For questions and comments about the quality of this book, please contact us at CustomerService@Harlequin.com.

Harlequin Enterprises ULC
22 Adelaide St. West, 41st Floor
Toronto, Ontario M5H 4E3, Canada
www.Harlequin.com

HarperCollins Publishers
Macken House, 39/40 Mayor Street Upper,
Dublin 1, D01 C9W8, Ireland
www.HarperCollins.com

Printed in U.S.A.

1 2 3 4 5 6 7 8 9 10 HDC 28 27 26 25

Billion-Dollar Brothers

The heat is on...and their hearts are at stake!

The name Nilson is synonymous with wealth, power... and rivalry! After an oppressively strict upbringing, brothers Arthur and Apollo only care about one competitor—each other. For years, their lives have been about being the best, no matter the cost...

As leaders in their fields, it seemed these billionaires had finally run out of battlefields. Until Apollo announces his divorce, and the clock starts ticking on a race to the altar!

But what will they find waiting at the finish line—just success, or something even sweeter?

Arthur Nilson has a plan. One wife, by the end of the year, and he'll have finally outshined his older brother. The only snag? Every dating app algorithm *hates* him. But when he takes his complaints direct to Pairably's CEO Gemma, he finds that love isn't always by-the-numbers...

Read Arthur and Gemma's story in

The CEO's Perfect Match

Apollo Nilson has a problem. His arranged marriage is officially doomed—all that's left is to sign the papers. But being back around his convenient wife ignites a spark that shines a new light on everything that's gone before. Is Kassandra his past...or the key to his future?

Read Apollo and Kassandra's story in

How Not to Divorce a Billionaire

Both available now!

Dear Reader,

Sometimes a character pops into your head. Other times, it is forced there by a story you previously told. When I wrote *The CEO's Perfect Match*, I had the hero's brother, Apollo, off-screen, except for the epilogue. But Apollo's not-so-ex-wife popped up in one of my favorite scenes ever. Suddenly I needed to tell Apollo and Kassie's love story.

Kassie Nilson married the love of her life and thought everything would be a fairytale, but found life second to Apollo's career too much. She stepped out on her own, but one hot night with her husband results in a nine-month surprise. Is it possible his promises to put her and their family first are real this time?

Billionaire Apollo Nilson has excelled at everything he's ever touched. Except his marriage to Kassie. He failed, hard. But when life gives him a second chance, can he make the changes necessary to convince his wife he can shine at marriage too?

Enjoy Apollo and Kassie's happily ever after!

Juliette Hyland

Juliette Hyland began crafting heroes and heroines in high school. She lives in Ohio with her Prince Charming, who has patiently listened to many rants regarding characters failing to follow the outline. When not working on fun and flirty happily-ever-afters, Juliette can be found spending time with her beautiful daughters, giant dogs or sewing uneven stitches with her sewing machine.

Books by Juliette Hyland

Harlequin Romance

If the Fairy Tale Fits...

Beauty and the Brooding CEO

Billion-Dollar Brothers

The CEO's Perfect Match

Falling for His Fake Date

Harlequin Medical Romance

Alaska Emergency Docs

One-Night Baby with Her Best Friend

Hope Hospital Surgeons

Dating His Irresistible Rival
Her Secret Baby Confession

Jet Set Docs

ER Doc's South Pole Reunion

San Diego Surgeons

Forbidden to the Millionaire Doc

Fake Dating the Vet

Visit the Author Profile page at Harlequin.com for more titles.

For Eve on your senior year. I am so proud of you.

PROLOGUE

SHOULD HE GO?

Apollo Nilson raised his glass with the next toast and made sure his smile was on point. He'd not expected an invitation to his brother's wedding and he'd had second, third and fourth thoughts about showing his face here. However, Arthur shaking his hand and introducing him to his new wife, Gemma, made the whole venture worth it.

"You don't have to rush off."

His heart pounded in his ears as he turned to face his wife. "I wasn't rushing—"

Kassie raised a brow. "Come now, Apollo. We haven't resided in the same home for two years, but I know you well enough to know you're thinking of setting that champagne flute down and hustling to the exit."

He could argue. But what was the point? The woman had known him to his core from nearly the second they'd met. His wife. The woman he'd let slip through his fingers.

There were days when it felt like yesterday that he had walked into a local writers' group hoping for a little camaraderie in a venture his family scorned. *No money in it. No fame. No glory.* Words his mother had shouted when she found his teenage wish list with *author* at the top.

They weren't technically true. Some people made it. But most never did. So he'd tried to bury the dream, but the words and stories seemed to come no matter what.

He'd slipped into the back of the group, sitting next to a young poetess. The woman who made words come alive in stanzas was the best thing about the night. They'd talked words and stories, and he'd felt whole for the first time in his life. There were moments when he thought that magic would be enough to carry them to forever.

But it wasn't.

The dream was dead, even though neither of them had filed the divorce papers.

He'd had colleagues who'd had near brawls before and during the divorce. But not him and Kass. They'd never fought. He'd let her slip into the background of his life. And the woman was such a saint; she'd never held it against him. She simply moved out and started over.

Without him.

It might have been easier if there had been arguments. If they weren't cordial at the few social events they still crossed paths at.

Still, in all but name, they were ex-husband and ex-wife. The only thing in his life he'd ever failed at.

"I don't belong here." *I'm lost without you.* At

least his brain managed to catch the words his heart nearly forced out.

And he wasn't lost. He just wasn't with her.

They'd parted amicably. Though to hear his parents tell it, his whole life had collapsed.

In a way, it has.

He swallowed that internal thought. His life was fine. He was at the top of his career.

Careers.

A bestselling author—under a pseudonym. The CEO of a company that made more money each day than some countries' yearly gross domestic production.

The only thing missing was the woman standing next to him for the first time in years.

Her hand rested on his elbow, and he wanted to capture the heat, force it into his soul. Reignite the fire that only she'd brought to his life.

"You do belong. You're Arthur's brother."

Brother. What did that title even mean?

They had been competitors from the day Arthur was born. And Apollo had won—always. The glory had been his. He'd basked in their parents' love and adoration—mostly. He'd spent more nights than not worried the pointed glares and cutting statements directed at Arthur would ricochet back to him. But they never had.

Until Kassie walked out.

Suddenly, the dark shadow Arthur had lived under was turned on him. His parents hadn't called him *son* since they'd found out his marriage was in trouble.

When the *scandal*, in his mother's words, broke that he and Kassie were mutually agreeing to separate, they'd cut him off. A lifetime spent trying to make them happy and then they'd just vanished. Like he'd committed some great sin.

He suddenly understood the pain that separation caused. A pain his brother had dealt with as a child and teenager.

It was why he was stunned Arthur had issued the invite. If he was a good big brother, he'd have realized how Arthur felt back then, would have been there for him, instead of slipping into the void himself.

A claw started to tighten around his throat. Anytime failure was close, his body reacted. He needed to leave. Needed to get to the office. There, he was a success. There, the feeling slipped to the background, even if it never fully faded.

"Kassie."

"Don't go." Her fingers squeezed his elbow and the claw vanished with her touch. "Don't go until you've had at least one dance with me. We used to be light on our feet together."

He had meetings. A book to send to his editor. A million things to do that weren't getting done here. But his tongue couldn't find the words for a polite decline.

Because I don't want to go.

Her fingers were laced through his, pulling him

toward the dance floor before his mind could find a way to step away. His heart leaped as he slid his arm around her waist.

Just one dance.

There was a magic in weddings. It was a space where everything seemed possible. Love lit up the world. But tomorrow he'd wake up without her.

She laid a hand against his shoulder, her soft smile only a little hesitant. "We have to move if we are actually dancing."

The light nervous giggle sent a thrill through him. How he'd missed her giggle. Her laughter. The light and color she brought into his world.

"Or we stand here and make people wonder what the hell we are doing." *What are we doing?*

"I think people may already be at that spot." Kassie swung her hips against his and immediately paused. "Your phone is buzzing."

The shadow she'd carried around the last months of their union dropped into place. "You didn't turn it off for your brother's wedding."

He'd never considered turning it off. He'd silenced it. His hand itched to reach in. He was always reachable. Always…

"I'm not answering it, Kassie." The words surprised him as he cupped her cheek, willing the sunshine she'd had in her gaze back into existence.

"But you want to." There were years of hurt baked into that statement. The vibrant poet he'd met that night had disappeared into the role of society wife.

The role her aristocratic parents had groomed her for. Technically members of the Swedish aristocracy, their link to the royal family was generations past. The connection granted them generational wealth and access to the echelons of the rich and upper class, where business was conducted at dinner parties but not much else.

That didn't stop her family from demanding she act like a woman destined for a crown.

Something she'd done so well, he hadn't noticed she was vanishing before his eyes.

Until she was gone.

"You want to. Don't you?" She took a tiny step back. Kassie shouldn't have had to ask the first time. And certainly not the second.

His mind was at war with his heart. His heart wanted to stay. Wanted to hold her close. Spin her around. Lose himself for just a bit.

Apollo's brain had no trouble reminding him that his agent was ready for his next book, and there were global economic reports coming in hourly. Responsibilities to handle. Responsibilities that seemed to pile at the door, pushing against everything. He'd once been so good at keeping all the plates balanced.

Except if that was true, there wouldn't be unsigned divorce papers with his name on them.

She took another step back. His heart overpowered his mind's recitations and he reached for her hand as he lifted the phone from his pocket. "I didn't turn it off for the wedding or my brother. But

I am turning it off for *you*." The claw strangled him as he slipped the phone into his pocket, not quite sure when the last time he had been unreachable was, until he spun her back into his arms.

The world and everything but her vanished in an instant. He could be unreachable for a few minutes with her.

"I like the tattoos." He caressed the flower on her wrist and spent a full second eyeing the geometric shape sliding down her shoulder and under the green dress. How far did it go? Once upon a time, he'd have known the answer.

"Thanks. My mother hates them." Kassie laughed and put her arms around his shoulders.

"Surely, that isn't the only reason you got them." He pulled her a little closer; this was the last time he was going to get to hold her. He needed every second she allowed.

A little pink colored her cheeks before she laid her head on his shoulder.

"Kassie." She'd grown up in an elite household with strict rules and expectations despite the very indirect line to actual royalty. She played by their rules. Expertly.

Hell, even though she'd fallen for the writer at her writers' club, she'd still had every plan to marry the billionaire economist they'd selected. The fact that he was one and the same was a universal gift he'd squandered.

"No. I didn't do it just to spite my mother. Nice

side effect, though." Her words were bright but he saw the pain behind them.

Her family had cut her off when she filed for divorce. He'd heard it through the constantly running gossip lanes. Her friends were mostly gone, too. Kassie had strength and she'd ended something rather than live separate lives—like her parents and so many others.

But he knew her heart. Knew that the tattoos were part of her and also a signal of her banishment. And he knew that Kassie wanted a family. Wanted to belong.

They'd talked about having a family. She'd wanted one, but he'd wanted to wait until he was more established. A ridiculous statement, but one he'd made over and over until she'd finally thrown back, "What more could you possibly want?"

And now that dream would belong to another man.

"Kassie." His throat closed as he tried to think of something to say. The many apologies she was owed; the desperation of his heart. All of the words strangled in his throat.

She lifted her head, her deep emerald gaze halting all the words that threatened to spill out as her soft lips brushed against his. "Tonight is just us. Nothing else. Not the past. Not the future. Just these dances. All right?"

"Dances?" Apollo pressed his lips to her forehead, careful not to linger more than a microsecond. "Does that mean I get another?"

"As many as you want." She beamed, then laughed as he spun her around, dipped her and brought her back into his arms.

"As many as you'll give me."

CHAPTER ONE

THE TWO LINES weren't disappearing. Neither was the plus sign. Or the word *pregnant* in the digital readout. Three tests. Three positive pregnancy tests.

Kassie wrapped her arms around herself and forced herself to look into the mirror. "Pregnant." The word echoed in the bathroom. The apartment she'd rented for her separation was supposed to be a launching point. A halfway house as she collected her thoughts and put the life she'd planned behind her.

Two years later, she was still here.

And she was pregnant with her husband's child.

Her goal, when she left, was to finally step out on her own. Make her own life instead of the one her parents crafted for her. A life she wanted. A life she thought she'd had a chance at with Apollo—before realizing the writer she'd fallen in love with was just as chained, if not more chained, to his desk than her father.

Her parents fought all the time when they were

home together. She and Apollo hadn't. She'd still loved him when she left.

It was the hardest moment of her life, but the loneliness was slowly killing her. If she was going to be lonely in the shadows, then why not step into the sun and create her own happiness?

She'd done some of it. Gotten a job. Her own place that was decorated with bright colors that no magazine would ever want to feature in fancy spreads. Her life was hers—sort of. She'd started down the path but had failed to make more than a few steps' progress.

A tiny sliver of her heart still craved the man who preferred business meetings to times with his wife. Still wanted to believe he'd pull his head out of his delectable derrière and come for her. A dream she should have let go so long ago.

Laying her hands over her still-flat belly, she sucked in a few breaths before forcing herself to breathe in through her nose and out through her mouth. Hyperventilating was not going to help the situation.

Pregnant.

Pregnant.

She'd wanted a family for as long as she could remember. She'd played with baby dolls long past the time her mother had deemed her too old for them. In fact, she'd only stopped because her mother had threatened to throw out the doll she loved most.

Pregnant.

This wasn't how it was supposed to work out.

She was supposed to have a partner. A person to support her. A partner she could lean on, so she didn't lose herself like her mother.

Her mother had played the societal role expected of her. And if she'd ever loved Kassie's father, that feeling had faded long ago. But she was still a lady. Still moved in the same circles, even if she and her husband hadn't resided in the same bed for two decades. That was the life Kassie had escaped.

She wanted a partner. A life of love.

For forever, she'd assumed that partner would be Apollo. When she moved out, she'd figured her dream would come true with a different person. A man who'd support the woman she'd found after she'd walked away from the man she loved, but who never saw her.

After two separate years, she couldn't seem to place another face in the mental image she had of herself growing old with.

Which was why the unsigned divorce papers were still clipped to the fridge with a magnet.

He hadn't signed his, either. They'd entered a stasis. A holding point. She should have ended it but every time she brought pen to paper, she hesitated.

Apollo, her Apollo, the one she'd met at a writers' group. The one that held her when her mother issued a vicious statement. The man who'd cheered when her poem was accepted into a small publication. That man was the one her heart still belonged to.

A man she'd wanted to believe was still hiding somewhere under the workload he'd set upon himself. A man who'd visited so rarely in their marriage. But the glimpses had kept her in the penthouse. Kept her rooted to a dream that never fully materialized no matter what she did.

She'd tried to be the perfect wife for so long. Years.

Up in the morning with him, so they could have breakfast together. Sure, he was usually already on his phone checking the markets. But she was there. She'd brought dinner to the office so often the secretaries knew to expect her.

Until they didn't.

It was a secretary who'd called to check when she hadn't shown up for a month. A secretary who'd quietly told her she'd miss her.

Back then, she'd believed Apollo would notice her absence. That he would say something. Ask why she'd stopped coming around. Miss spending even that hour a day with her.

When it hit the six-month mark, she'd moved her stuff out. And he hadn't called.

That was the day that nearly broke her. But she'd picked herself up. Dusted herself off. Created a life she'd never dreamed of.

Most days she ignored the tiny ache that Apollo wasn't beside her. The flame of hope she'd kept lit for so long refused to flame out, though.

Which was why she'd been so happy when he'd shown up to Arthur and Gemma's wedding. Why she'd moved, when she saw him getting ready to leave. Why she'd asked him to dance. And then kept him on the floor until they were two of the final guests and it would be weird to stay any longer.

But neither had been willing to walk away. So they'd come to her place. They'd danced in her living room. Laughed. Joked.

It was her Apollo. The author. The sweet man who paid attention to her. The one who made her feel loved. The one who made her feel seen.

They'd fallen into bed at her place. Everything perfection. A unification that felt like finally coming home.

A magical memory. Right up until she woke up next to an empty pillow. No note. No text. No goodbye.

She'd sworn she wouldn't be the first to break that silence. Sworn that this time she was not reaching out. Kassie was always the one reaching out. The peacemaker. The one who put aside her feelings to make others comfortable.

She apologized to her father when he didn't attend *her* wedding. Told her mother she was sorry *her* marriage didn't work out. Not that it mattered. They'd cast her aside.

Kassie crafted her path now.

She was not supposed to be the one who caved now.

There were options. But she knew, as she ran her thumb over the tiny clump of cells that would be her daughter or son, that she was having this baby.

"I have to reach out to Apollo." *Ugh.* She wiped a tear from her cheek, very aware that there was no way to blame hormones for the waterworks. This was not supposed to be the way she started her family.

She looked at her phone. What were the right words? Did she send them now or wait?

No. Waiting wasn't an option. She grabbed her phone and put in the first thing she could think of.

We need to talk.

Before she could doubt herself, Kassie hit Send. Apollo read the message immediately.

Of course he did. He was tied to his phone. It was how most of the conversations had happened in their marriage. A text from her. A response from him. Usually an apology that he'd be late, again.

The man was successful beyond most people's wildest dreams. A Nobel in Economic Sciences winner, a billionaire investor, even a bestselling mystery writer—though he wrote under a pen name so no one knew.

Everything he touched turned to gold…except their marriage.

She'd once joked with him that he didn't know how to have fun. He'd laughed and said that was what mystery writing was. She'd playfully punched him and said no, that he'd turned that into a full-time job, too.

He'd frowned and said that he didn't know what she meant about fun, then.

In another world she'd have found a way to get him into therapy. To force him to examine what he wanted from life and find happiness in something that wasn't the accolades that continued to pour in.

Maybe if she were an accolade, he'd want her.

A conversation she'd nearly had toward the end when he'd showed up late for dinner for the hundredth time that year. Instead, she'd played the role she'd taken on. Perfect, unbothered wife. She'd chatted, they'd laughed and she'd done her best to pretend that the little pieces of affection that came her way were enough.

Once more she'd let the question die away in kisses and a night spent with him worshipping her body. The bedroom was one area where they'd never struggled.

Which was why she was standing here waiting for him to respond.

The minutes ticked by and she bit the inside of her cheek. He was not going to ignore her. Not after she'd broken the promise she'd made not to reach out.

Not when she was carrying his child.

As if he heard her across an invisible mental line, her phone buzzed.

Not today. Lots of meetings.

Lots of meetings. That was his life. Hell, she'd

had more dinners with him in his office than she'd shared with him in their penthouse apartment.

Something snapped. This was not happening. He was not putting her off. No. Not today.

She was not waiting for his schedule to open up. Kassie had spent far too much of her life accommodating others. She needed to talk to him. So that was what was happening.

Right now.

"I don't like any of these options. The markets are going to hold." Apollo didn't acknowledge Henry's frustration. His chief of the North American division didn't quite catch the sigh on the edge of his lips.

"Sir—"

"It will hold." Apollo crossed his arms. He knew numbers and economies better than almost anyone in the world. And he was right.

I wasn't last month.

No. That wasn't true. He would have been right. If he'd gotten the news. If he hadn't been worshipping Kassie's body. The first time in his career he hadn't picked up the phone as a market tumbled.

Tumbled, not crashed, but investors were hesitant by nature. He'd made several adjustments in the investment firm's plan and earned back everyone's money, plus some, in three days. A fact that several investors still hadn't appreciated.

If we hadn't lost the money we'd have made even more.

He didn't appreciate the look of hesitation on his director's face. "Do you have something to add?"

Henry swallowed. There was a hint of rebellion there. The man had goals. Dreams.

It was like looking into a mirror. Once upon a time, he'd stood in front of someone who'd thought his analysis was inaccurate. He'd proved them wrong.

Apollo had bought the man's company when it crashed a few years later. A satisfying day indeed.

Henry wasn't proving him wrong today, but it might happen in the future. The man was going to open his own firm one day. Then he could sit in the chair and make the decisions. Until then, he answered to Apollo. Full stop.

Henry straightened and swallowed. It was a tell. One he needed to work on. "I think there's a good chance this backfires. I think there's likely to be a downturn in the Asian markets. The hints are there."

"Hints? Hints are just a way to keep you from jumping to something big. Indicators are what we look for." One thing Apollo had learned over time was that people had a tendency to worry first. That reaction cost money. So did recklessness. But the last thing Apollo Nilson was was reckless. He was the best at this game.

Even if it was a game that brought him little joy. He was good. Better than good. That was what he focused on. The success. The accolades. The awards.

"I, of course, trust your word." Henry made eye contact, but his gaze shifted just a hint.

"I do." Apollo waited until the man's gaze found his and refused to look away. No concern. He was in charge.

Then he stood and headed out of the conference room. He had another meeting in fifteen minutes. Another meeting after that. And then another.

Meetings doing nothing to drive away the thoughts of his wife's text.

We need to talk.

Four little words. Four tiny words. Twelve letters. And a million meanings.

Did she want to finally finalize their divorce? Or talk about the night of Arthur's wedding?

In his dreams he still saw her, draped over him, perfect breasts, long, dark hair streaming down her shoulders. That geometric tattoo ran from the tip of her shoulder to just above her enticing derrière. He'd traced it with his fingers. With his tongue.

And left without waking her the next morning. His neck heated at that shame. He should have stayed. Should have at least said good morning.

But then what?

They were all but divorced. And he'd had to right the ship after he hadn't answered the phone. They'd made a mistake…though a tiny whisper from his heart had questioned if he was slinking out before she woke so he didn't have to hear her say it.

"Sir!" Emilio, his uptight assistant, raced toward him. Whatever was happening probably wasn't an emergency but the man seemed incapable of seeing anything other than the dullest note as DEFCON one. More than once, he'd told the man that a simple email or phone call fixed nearly everything.

The man was efficient, dependable and had a work ethic to match his. But over the past year, Apollo had realized Emilio was simply incapable of not panicking at least twice a week. The only reason he kept him on was he never complained about the long hours, never asked for a vacation or demanded a life. He worked as hard as Apollo... something no other assistant had managed in his twelve years in this office.

"Emilio—"

"She just barged into your office. I told her you were busy, but she is *sitting* in your chair." Emilio shook his head. "I told her I was calling security, but she said to get you or get out."

His assistant ran a hand through his short blond hair then looked at the appendage as though it had acted on its own accord.

"Your hair still looks fine." Emilio and his hair. One of the other assistants routinely joked that it was his first love. There was no way the man had a love life. He was at the office as much as Apollo... which meant always.

Hell, even the plants in his home were fake. The ones left behind after Kassie walked out died within weeks. Another reminder that she wasn't there. That she'd done something because it made him happy and he hadn't even realized that they needed caring for.

Just like he hadn't cared for her.

"She took over your desk." The man pursed his lips. "Security is on the way."

"Then the interloper will be gone shortly." One did not work in business without seeing some unusual things. People got upset about not getting jobs, about getting fired, about life in general. This was the first time a disgruntled person had reached his office, but he wasn't there. Security would handle it.

His phone buzzed and he looked at the text then back at Emilio. "Call off security. Now." He could make that call but his feet were already moving past his assistant. His brain already shutting out everything besides getting to his office.

"Sir?"

He heard the question in Emilio's voice but didn't turn around. "I said call them off!"

His assistant had never met Kassie. Never ordered food for him and his wife to eat over his desk. Something they'd done at least three times a week until the year before she'd walked out.

It was only when she'd gone that he'd realized the dinner meetings had fallen away.

Why is she here?

Her text this morning only said they needed to talk. But it hadn't seemed urgent.

Or maybe I wanted to push it off.

Kassie was easygoing. She didn't make a fuss. It was the reason their union had lasted as long as it had. At least according to the therapist he saw exactly twice. The man had wanted to schedule him for weekly sessions. But what was the point?

He was who he was.

"That is right. I'm not leaving." Her voice was strong as it came through the door, but he could hear the pain in the words.

Flinging the door open, he met his head of security's gaze. Annalise knew Kassie and she'd clearly gotten the message that they needed to vacate. Not that he thought Annalise would toss Kassie out. She sent him a glare as she pushed the guards out the door.

The woman had been with him for almost a decade. She knew her position was safe. And he knew she didn't approve of being asked to throw out his ex-wife.

The divorce papers aren't signed.

That was a technicality. One he did not want to focus on too much.

"Sorry. Emilio doesn't know you." Apollo started toward her. She wasn't in his chair; maybe Emilio had overstated, or maybe she'd gotten up. Either way, he wanted to be closer to her, though he wasn't sure what he planned to do when he got to her side.

"It's fine." She shrugged like security arriving to throw her out wasn't a huge deal.

How many times had he heard that phrase during

their marriage? How many times had he accepted it at face value?

Hell, until he'd come home to a flat empty of her things, he'd believed everything was fine.

"It's not fine. I'm sorry."

She shrugged—again. Defeat heavy on her shoulders as she leaned against his desk. "We need to talk."

"I'll sign the divorce papers." The words shredded his soul. But he couldn't stand the pain on her face. She deserved so much more than the stasis they were occupying.

"That's not why I'm here." She let out a breath. "Maybe it should be. But it isn't."

He started toward her again, but she held up a hand. Why was she here if not for the divorce?

"I don't want anything from you." She looked at the floor then back at him, "Not true."

Those words nearly sent him to his knees. Whatever she wanted, he'd do it.

"I don't expect anything. I know—" she gestured to the desk "—I know this is first."

"Meaning?" None of her words registered in the pain of those sentences. He'd failed her. So many times.

"I'm pregnant." She crossed her arms. Uncrossed them, then recrossed them. "It's yours. I—I haven't seen anyone else."

They were divorced—basically. It wasn't his business whom she was seeing. But she wasn't seeing anyone. That knowledge breathed light into the nearly flamed-out ball of hope his soul refused to let die.

He'd seen no one since she'd walked out. He had no desire to find anyone else. He'd fumbled the best thing and now she was here. In front of him. *Pregnant.*

"Pregnant." The word felt funny on his tongue. Kassie wanted a family. He'd never given too much thought to this moment, but her telling him he was going to be a father while oceans seemingly stood between them was not the way this was supposed to go.

"Pregnant." He repeated the word for no good reason.

"This wasn't planned. I… I get that."

Apollo moved without thinking; the break at the end of her words nearly crushed him.

He reached for her, pulling her into his arms, grateful she didn't pull back. "Sometimes plans change."

"Right." She let out a tiny hiccup then stepped back. "Sorry."

Without her in his arms, Apollo was lost. But she didn't need to hear that. "Please don't apologize."

"I meant it. You don't need to be involved. But I am keeping the baby." Her left hand moved to cover her still-flat belly. "We can put a new clause in the divorce."

"I'll be involved." The words seemed to dance as they flew from his mouth. He hadn't thought this through. Didn't know why he'd said it so certainly. Still, the words felt so right. Why?

He had no idea how to be a father. He certainly had no plan to lean into the lessons his parents instilled. Love—or what passed for it—only issued when one achieved. A brief positive response followed by a reminder not to rest on any laurels.

The fact that it hadn't destroyed him and Arthur was nearly a miracle.

He also had no idea how to right the broken path he and Kass now walked.

"I'll figure it out." There were meetings and more meetings. His life was scheduled from the second he woke to the second he fell into his bed.

He didn't know anything about parenting. His own parents weren't winning any awards, that was for damn sure. But there were books and blogs and academic articles. He was more than capable of picking up the correct skills.

Right?

"Apollo." Kassie bit her lip. "You spend fifteen hours a day here."

There was no anger in her voice. Maybe if there were, the words wouldn't cut.

The acceptance. The truth—it stole the wind from his lungs, the words from his lips.

During their marriage he was here more than at home. Forcing himself to earn more. To keep going. It was how he was raised. Achieve or be nothing.

He'd doubled down since she'd left. There were responsibilities here. His responsibilities. It was the only thing left now that she was gone and his parents had cut him off.

But he could find a way to balance. A way to succeed here and at fatherhood. Couldn't he?

A knock echoed in the silence and Emilio stepped in without waiting. "Sir, you have a meeting."

Balance. His first test. "I'm going to be late. Just tell them to wait. I need a few minutes."

His wife's face fell.

"Not necessary." Kassie shook her head. "I was leaving. I just..." Her emerald gaze gripped his. "I simply needed you to know."

"Kassie, wait."

"The clients are getting angry." Emilio looked at the tablet that was stuck to him at all times. "But I can probably push them off for a bit longer."

"No." The word left his lips, and Kassie didn't hide the look of pain fast enough.

Damn. He hadn't meant for it to sound so certain. So final. He needed to meet with the clients but they could wait a bit longer.

"Kassie—"

She didn't look back as she passed Emilio and went out the door.

The claw wrapped around his throat. The first test...failed. How was he supposed to do this?

"I spoke with Roger. He is furious with the delay. I may have let slip that you were in here working on something to wow him." Emilio winked. "Figured that would keep him in his seat rather than bullying his way down here."

"I don't have anything to wow Roger." He kept his gaze rooted to the door, willing Kassie to walk back through it. Knowing she was gone.

"You'll think of something. You always do." Emilio tapped a few things out on his tablet. "I'll go let him know you're on your way."

The door closed and Apollo looked at his oak desk. It was a statement piece. Worth more than the rest of the office furniture all together.

You'll come up with something.

A motto he'd heard more than once in his career. Apollo the fixer. Apollo the brilliant. Apollo the man to go to. All lines he'd heard regularly. All lines he'd secretly craved hearing.

Apollo…the father.

That was a tag he didn't know how to wear. But he was going to do his best to figure it out.

CHAPTER TWO

"I JUST DON'T KNOW." Bridgette flipped through the images on the tablet.

Her mother laid a hand on her knee. "You don't have to pick this moment. You could ask David."

The bride let out a tiny huff. "These are the flowers for my bouquet. David's been involved in everything." Bridgette smiled. "Which is nice, because some of my friends have different experiences."

Kassie kept her face blank. She'd started working as a wedding planner after leaving the penthouse. Her parents were appalled—that she worked at all—at least according to her brother, the only member of the family still talking with her.

Most of the *friends* she'd had slipped away when she left Apollo. They vanished completely when she started working. Appalled for reasons she refused to understand.

She loved the life she'd created. None of it had been given to her.

She'd had to convince Signa to hire her. Had to prove herself since she had no résumé. She'd done it by working harder than anyone with little praise.

Something that would pay off when Signa finally made her partner.

She'd told her it would happen soon. Technically, she and Liza were up for it at the same time, but Kassie was better. Signa had told her that. Basically.

This was her place. Her expertise. The life she'd crafted for herself.

"Maybe something lighter?" Bridgette said the words, but the bride wasn't really paying attention. Her thoughts were far outside this room.

Kassie turned the page on the tablet she used in the office to another bouquet set. "These are much softer. But if you want to wait…or ask David. He's a good sounding board."

"I *don't* want to ask David's mom. I love how involved he is, but this should be a surprise." Bridgette let out a sigh as she flipped through the flowers on the screen.

During the past two years, more than one bride had sat opposite her, looking at the door, hoping their partner would walk through. She'd been one of them.

It was a red flag she should have talked over with Apollo, rather than just accepting his busy schedule. At the time, it was easy to look past. Easy to believe it was just a minor thing.

That the writer she loved was just sticking it out at the company until he felt comfortable stepping away and writing full-time. A dumb thought then.

Apollo had enough to never work another day in his life the day she met him.

Yet, he was chained to his desk…willingly.

"It is understandable to want something to be a surprise." Kassie leaned across the desk. Wedding planning was rife with emotions. Good and bad. "Tell me why the bouquet is making you weepy."

Often it was just stress. More than one couple focused in on one tiny element. Put all their *stress coins*, as she liked to call them, on that one item.

"Daddy loved flowers." Bridgette wiped away a tear. "I've known for years he wouldn't be here. Wouldn't get to do some of the traditions. But he'd have loved picking flowers with me."

"You two could even have sat in the same room for it." Bridgette gave her mother a watery wink.

"We may not have been together, but we were united in our love for you." Bridgette's mother pushed a hair behind her ear. "That was one thing we never wavered on. Let's head home. Get all our feelings out then come back. Right?" The woman's soft gaze turned to Kassie.

"Right. We're only looking at styles here in the office. That way we know which florist is best to book. I'll send you this file. Look at it at home with tissues and tea."

Bridgette bit her lip before offering a quick, unnecessary apology and taking her leave.

When the door to her office shut, Kassie leaned back in her chair, sucking in deep breaths. She had two more meetings with brides and grooms this afternoon. She couldn't smudge her makeup.

No one wanted a weepy wedding planner.

Her life wasn't heading in the direction she'd expected. Hell, that was an understatement. She was pregnant. And Apollo couldn't spare a single meeting.

She pinched her eyes closed. That wasn't fair. She'd quite literally sprung herself on him.

After he didn't answer my text.

No. He answered. Just not in the way I wanted.

Either way. She'd given him exactly zero time to adjust to the idea that he was going to be a father.

That wasn't overly fair, either. To Apollo, or their child.

He'd said he wanted to be involved. That he would be involved. Rather than accept that, she'd told him that she knew his work came first. It did, but that didn't mean Apollo couldn't be involved.

Bridgette wanted her dad. Something no one this side of the mortal coil could offer. Her mother had said little regarding the demise of her union with Bridgette's father, but it was clear they'd not had any love lost between them. It was also clear that given the option, she'd have done anything to make sure her daughter had both her parents available to see her big day.

Because that was what parents did. They acted in the best interest of their kids.

Or it was what good parents did, according to

the movies and television shows she'd binged growing up.

Her own father had missed her wedding. Ironic, given that he'd orchestrated the whole arrangement. An arrangement she'd dreaded until she'd walked in and laid eyes on Apollo. The mystery writer she'd gone out to dinner with twice. The man who'd asked about her poetry and laughed with such ease.

She wanted to believe that she would have told her parents no, if it wasn't Apollo at that dinner. But she knew that wasn't true. Her parents raised her to be a socialite. A wife to a man of wealth and influence. A mirror of their own union.

The fact that she met a man she was desperately in love with at the altar was a miracle. The fact that he was more like her father than the writer she'd fallen for was a truth she hadn't wanted to accept when she sat alone at planning events.

Apollo mirrored the man she'd grown up with. *Workaholic* didn't begin to cover the drive her husband had. The man lived for accolades and there was no award for husband of the year. So she slipped further and further back on his seemingly ever-growing to-do list.

All her life she'd offered the apology first. Smoothed the issue. But today she'd simply dropped a bomb and walked out.

Ugh. None of that mattered. She was carrying their child. Maybe they weren't together but she could set aside her frustration, and heartache, for her little bean.

"Sir! You can't just barge in." Her assistant's shouted words echoed through the closed door. Claire had turned away more than one angry mother-of-the groom or jilted lover. This business was hardly dull. At least it was something to drag her mind away from her husband.

Kassie turned, ready to order the intruder from her office.

"Kassie." Apollo held up his hands in surrender as soon as he opened the door. "We need to talk."

"I have meetings." She bit her lip and looked at Claire. There was an hour before the next couple arrived, but she wasn't ready to deal with her husband. Not yet.

"Cancel them."

How dare he! "Why? You didn't want to cancel your meeting this morning. You think your work is more important than mine."

It wasn't a question. She hadn't worked when they were married. She'd made her life revolve around his. His schedule. His needs.

She'd continued to write poetry. Even published under a pen name, so as not to embarrass her parents. But it wasn't a nine-to-five.

Her work here was important. It didn't make millions every few minutes but it made people happy. Brought them joy. And she was good at it. In two years, she'd gone from an apprentice to senior planner. Soon, she'd be a partner. An achievement all on her own.

"I didn't say it wasn't important."

"But you aren't arguing the point. Are you, Apollo?" She crossed her arms. She didn't want to argue. Part of her wasn't even sure why she was.

For the entirety of their marriage, she'd kept the peace. Playing the same role she'd played in her family. She'd wanted him to cancel his day for her and he had. Or he'd canceled a few things because Apollo Nilson did not have a free hour in his schedule.

But it suddenly wasn't enough.

"We aren't here to compare wins."

Because you always win.

She hated even thinking that.

Doesn't make it false.

"You blindsided me, Kass. I didn't respond well. I know that. I accept it and I am sorry. But the last thing I expected was for you to walk in and tell me you're pregnant."

Claire let out a sound and moved to close the door.

"Don't bother, Claire. Clearly, my husband doesn't care who knows I'm carrying his baby." Apollo paled. He'd outed her pregnancy; stolen her choice in making the decision.

At least he seemed to realize the mistake.

"I'm sorry." He pursed his lips. "I'm saying that a lot today."

"I believe the count is less than five. So that hardly equals a lot, Apollo. Why are you here?" She had just gotten herself under control before he arrived—mostly. She'd made the decision to reach back out. To coparent well. But she wasn't quite ready.

That did not give her an excuse to be petty, though.

Maybe it does.

Her brain really wanted to punish him. That wasn't fair. She'd known who he was when she married him. A man driven to success. She just thought she'd be on the same pedestals as those successes. It had taken far too long to realize she wasn't a shiny trophy, so she couldn't be a priority.

Apollo looked to Claire then to Kassie. "Kass, do you have an appointment?"

"Yes. The bride will be here any minute." Claire answered for her.

Her assistant didn't know what was going on. Kassie had never mentioned her husband. Never mentioned what was, or wasn't, between them. But she was standing on business.

"Fine. I will schedule some time on your calendar." He turned his attention to Claire. "I assume you can find me some?"

Claire's dark gaze met hers. She was not going to answer until Kassie gave the affirmative.

Kassie gave a short nod. At least if it was scheduled, she could have her thoughts written down. A plan in place. Emotions in check.

So far today they'd both barged into each other's offices. Not the best scenario for either.

"We need to talk, Kass." *Kass.*

No one called her that. Technically, no one called

her Kassie, either. Only Apollo shortened her name. And Kass was his soft nickname. The one he whispered in her ear when he held her. The one that once nearly equaled happily ever after.

"Get on my schedule." She'd replayed telling him that so many times in the two years they'd been apart. This was supposed to be her big satisfying moment.

The moment that made him realize how much she hated that he'd scripted her into his life. The satisfying comeuppance.

Hollow didn't begin to touch the description of how it really felt.

Apollo nodded. "Of course." Then he stepped out.

She could go after him. Tell him that there was another hour before her next client. But Kassie's feet were rooted to the ground.

He'd canceled three meetings to come over here. Made sure all his clients were taken care of. He'd expected Kassie to do the same.

Why?

Because she always had.

That was a hard truth. In an academic way, he'd known that Kass fit herself into his schedule. Dinners at the office. Vacations cut short or canceled because he needed to see to some client. Communication more through texts than anything else.

Today that truth smacked him directly in the face.

She'd challenged him about whether his job was more important than hers. And he'd almost said yes.

Apollo closed his eyes and leaned his head back against the headrest of his Bugatti. His phone buzzed. A client wanting something. He should reach for it, but his hand stayed out of his pocket.

Apollo sucked in a deep breath. Trying to push away the claw climbing up his throat. He could return the phone call. Other people weren't on call constantly and it was fine.

Don't rest on your laurels. His mother's harsh tone echoed in his head.

Breathe.

He should head back to the office, but he couldn't move. He'd almost told his wife that his work was more important. He'd barely caught the words.

Who did that?

Me. The same way I didn't realize how rough Arthur had it.

He ran a finger under his tie but loosening it did nothing to stop the claw.

Kass's work was important. Of course it was. And her nameplate read Senior Planner. A big accomplishment.

And he hadn't known.

Wedding planning. It was not something he'd have guessed. Though maybe he should have. His wife loved happiness, color and love.

She'd never worked while they were married. She'd authored poetry and filled the apartment with arts-and-crafts projects that she loved. But she'd never set foot in an office that wasn't his. She'd never even mentioned wanting something like that.

I never asked.

He was positive there wasn't another meeting. At least not right then. Her assistant Claire was covering for her. Like a good assistant should. She'd offered him time tomorrow.

Tomorrow. Twenty-four hours. More than enough time for them to collect themselves. But also, forever away.

He'd started to argue but then accepted the lunch hour. However, Apollo was not waiting until tomorrow. Still, her office was hers. He owed her the ability to control her own schedule during the working day.

Particularly since he'd outed her pregnancy. Another flop on this day where he'd made exactly zero right moves.

He'd simply wait until her day was over. He could work from the car. Apollo grabbed his phone and instructed his assistant to direct all calls to his phone. He answered a few questions. The pressure on his neck started to lift—a bit.

One day working out of the office would be fine. A mini vacation, sort of. Or not really at all. But different.

After checking a few emails, he drove to a bakery. Grabbed a cookie and then drove back to the parking lot as a couple walked into the office. He was going to wait. And when she walked out, he was going to be there. With an apology cookie.

Kass had more than earned it.

His head was bent, reading another email on the tiny screen on his phone. He'd taken all his calls in the car. Answered more than fifty emails and looked over the outline he was working on for his mystery. The one that was due in a few months that was already behind schedule. Not terribly behind, but enough that it gave him a little pinch of worry anytime he looked at his home office door.

Kass hadn't come out yet, but he'd been productive.

Not in the office.

It was a weird feeling. Apollo lived there. But today proved things could get done without him sitting in the c-suite. It was strange to find that it was possible to manage outside of it.

Yes, he'd gone on business trips. But those were different. He'd never worked from home. Never taken a day where he was out of the office.

The company hadn't fallen apart. The anxiety that kept him rooted to the desk hadn't reared its ugly head more than once or twice.

Henry could step in to any meetings he didn't want to take in person. The man was more than willing. As long as Apollo kept an eye on things, he could work from anywhere.

A realization he should have easily made. Better ultra late than never.

Right?

Claire stepped out of the office, her purse over her shoulder. She looked directly at the tinted windows of the Bugatti. Then she pulled out a phone and started texting. No doubt warning Kassie that he was out here.

His phone buzzed a second later.

May as well come in.

He grabbed the cookie. A tiny goodwill offering. One so tiny he was instantly aware that he should have done something different.

What was the right thing to bring to a sorry-I-acted-like-an-ass-when-you-told-me-you-were-pregnant meeting? Jewelry?

Whatever the right answer was, all he had was the cookie.

He walked to the entrance. Claire didn't leave her perch by the door.

"I won't blame you if you want to stay. But I promise she is safe with me."

"Physically. Maybe. But emotionally, is that true?" Claire tilted her head, then sighed as her phone buzzed and she read the note. "She ordered me to go home. But she's the best boss I've ever had. She works harder here than anyone else. Do not hurt her."

Apollo didn't know what to say to that. So he nodded and opened the door.

Kass as a boss. He'd have never considered that a possibility. Though her being the best boss made a weird bit of sense.

Her office door was open, but she wasn't in there. "Kass?"

"Back here."

He followed her call down the hall to a well-designed kitchen area. She was pulling food from the fridge. Pastries and cake lined the small table. He was already aware that the cookie was a poor offering but when she had access to this, it was the definition of paltry.

"We change out our cake samples at the end of the day. I usually have the interns do it, but I'm trying to figure out if there is any pattern to what people like. What is gone more. Trend analysis to forecast things we should see coming or going." She looked at the tray, counted a few things and made a note on her tablet.

Interns. Trend analysis.

Words he never expected to hear come from his wife's mouth. She was so sure of herself. It was incredibly sexy to see.

"Today isn't the best data. I had two couples who chose the very first thing they tried so if you want something..." She gestured to the table and then went to the cabinet and grabbed a teacup.

"I brought a cookie." He held up the box. "It has a lot of pink frosting on it. Arthur recommended it. We don't talk much but I guess Gemma likes the place."

"It's nice that you're chatting."

He shrugged. "Nothing deep. The cookie was safe conversation."

He and Arthur had reconnected. A little. It still felt stilted, or maybe it was him. He was surprised Arthur had wanted him at his wedding. Stunned that he kept the lines of communication open after.

It was a gift he didn't deserve.

Big brothers were supposed to protect their little brothers. He'd failed him. Many times.

Just like he'd failed Kass.

"Well, reconnection has to start somewhere. Safe conversations are the best. Thank you for the cookie." Kassie took the cookie box then poured hot water over the tea diffuser. "Arthur knows the bakery because Gemma's friend owns it. She was going to set it up in London but was looking for a change of scenery and came here. I don't have any coffee made, sorry."

Speaking of safe conversations.

"I didn't come to talk sweets." She knew that. He just didn't know where to go with this.

"I figured you weren't sitting in the car out there all day to talk pastries." She walked past him, holding the teacup and bakery box.

"Your assistant saw me." He didn't bother to make it sound like a question.

Kassie chuckled.

How he'd missed that sound.

"No. Both grooms and one bride all talked about the car. The Bugatti Tourbillion started delivery this year. And only 250 are ever being produced. No one expected to see one in this parking lot." Kassie moved behind her desk and sat down.

"Wasn't aware you were interested in the car." He loved fast cars. It was one of the few perks of his wealth he really relished.

"I'm not. But I heard about it many times today." She lifted the tea to her lips.

His eyes followed the motion, honed in on the subtle lipstick she was wearing. He was almost a little jealous of the cup.

"Why are you here, Apollo? Why stay all day for me?" She let out a tiny sigh as she set the teacup down.

For me.

What a punch in the gut. There was no heat in the questions. No anger. She deserved better.

Their child deserved better.

"You're pregnant." He slipped into the chair across from her.

"I am. I scheduled my first appointment at the clinic. It's next week."

"I'll be there."

Kassie looked at the teacup, then her bright gaze met his. "We both know something more important will come up. I want you to be involved. Our child deserves that. But—"

"No buts, Kass, I'll be there. Just send me the time." *Something more important.* She was his wife. Carrying his child. It shouldn't be possible for her to think that something more important would drop.

But I never put her first.

Another realization that had popped in while he

was in the car. Yes, she'd said it in his office. His ears had heard it but until she'd dismissed him, his brain hadn't made the connection.

Another failure to add to the list building up today.

"Kass—"

Kassie bit her lip. "Please stop calling me that." She took a deep breath that he was nearly positive was so she didn't let out a sob.

"Kass." He swallowed. "Kassie, or would you prefer Kassandra?" Only he shortened her name. She'd joked about it on their first date. Their real one. Not the one arranged by their parents. The one at a local coffee shop where they'd chatted about books and movies. A magical night that had made him feel whole and seen for the first time. In that place he was simply Apollo. Not trying to achieve anything.

He'd called her Kassie by accident and she'd grinned. Said no one called her anything other than Kassandra but that she liked how it rolled so easily off his tongue.

She'd told him how her mother had demanded nothing but the best of her daughter. No mistakes… and nicknames were mistakes. It was logic that was beyond his comprehension. But he'd told her his own parents were the same. Demanding. Seeing only success and failure with no shades of gray in between.

"Kassandra." She shrugged. "It just… I don't know. I just need it to be Kassandra."

He nodded, unwilling to trust his voice in this moment. They'd bonded over their shared childhood experiences on those first dates, and she'd been Kassie or Kass to him ever since. The one thing he hadn't let change from those initial dates.

Now she was putting a hard boundary in place. One he'd respect even though it cut through his soul.

"I'll send you the time."

"And I *will* be there." He'd make sure nothing got in front of this.

Kassie looked down. "When our child is born, don't make promises you can't keep, all right? That is the only thing I'm asking."

Her father had had two children because it was what was expected of him societally. A boy and a girl. Her brother was a hedge fund manager in New York City. He'd not come home for the wedding. Or any other family function.

And Kassie's father hadn't come to their wedding, either. He'd gone to a business meeting in Prague that had "run late." Their child, *his* child, was never going to feel the things Kassie had.

And their mother wasn't, either. Not anymore. He'd failed at his marriage. The only thing in his life where he'd tasted the bitterness of defeat.

He'd accepted it…though he waited for her to sign the divorce papers. He wasn't accepting defeat now. He could make this work. He *would* make this work.

"I'll be there, Kassandra. Every moment of this pregnancy, I will be there."

"Apollo—"

"I will be there."

She shrugged. "Part of me wants to believe that."

"And the other part?" He leaned forward in the chair.

"The other part is aware that you can't be the best father. There's no award or accreditation for it, so you won't put our child first. Just like there's no award for best husband."

He blew out a breath. "Don't ask questions you don't want answers to, I guess."

She opened her mouth, then closed it. Her jeweled gaze met his and she smiled, but it didn't reach her eyes. "Thank you for the cookie. I need to close up. Have a good night, Apollo and thank you, for waiting today. It means more than you know."

He'd been dismissed. As much as he wanted to argue, as much as he wanted to stay and do whatever closing up meant in a wedding planner's office, he didn't want to press himself upon her any more than he already had today.

"Send me the time. And if you need anything before the doctor's appointment." He stood and started for the door, hoping she'd ask him to stay. But the request didn't come.

He made it to the car and looked back at the office. He'd never gotten to know his wife. Not really. That was his mistake. And one he needed to fix.

Now.

CHAPTER THREE

"I UNDERSTAND THAT the clients are going to feel this change, Emilio. I am the CEO of The Nilson Group. But I am making some changes." Apollo looked at his watch; he had a plan for the day that needed to get started.

There is no award.

His wife's words hung in his soul. There might not be an award for best husband and father, but he was planning on metaphorically winning one anyway. He was the best at everything else, so he was going to make sure he was the best at fatherhood and being a husband.

All that meant he had to trust his gut with the company right now. Scary as it was.

"I think Henry will be a good substitute for that meeting, if the client insists on having a one-on-one. I need to shift some things. But I am still very reachable. Clearly." He had no intention of being out of pocket, just out of the office.

Change was a scary word. One that had sent panic down his spine more than once last night.

This was not a mission he could fail. Which

meant change had to happen. He'd figure out the new balancing act. Find a way to make everything work seamlessly.

Kassandra deserved that.

"If any client is rude to you, you let me know. I'll cut them loose at once. But effective immediately, I am working from home most days." It was a decision he'd made sitting in the car.

Nothing had fallen apart. In fact, besides his assistant, no one had even noticed really. Many clients preferred video teleconferencing. And more than half his staff worked remotely or in another nation. There was no reason for him to be chained to his desk.

That didn't mean he wasn't giving his all to his company.

For his entire childhood, his parents had warned him that giving less than 110 percent was giving in to failure mindset.

Failure mindset.

Who said that to a child?

His parents.

Apollo had no idea how to parent. He had read a ton of parenting blogs the previous night. A little bit of everything. All he knew right now was he was damn sure his and Kassie's child got his best from this moment forward.

No. Not his best. Better than his best. He was going to be perfect.

And right now, that meant being there for his child's mother.

My wife.

He swallowed as the image of Kassie danced through his mind.

"I understand, sir. I do. I'm just not sure…"

He could tell Emilio was probably frowning on the other end of the phone. This was a shift for his assistant, too. But Apollo knew he could rise to the occasion. He was going to have to.

"You don't have to be sure. There will be adjustments. For me. For you. For the clients."

The claw that he'd finally put to bed last night wrapped around his throat. He was not going to give in to it. Not right now. He had other things to handle. His clients would be fine. Everything was going to be fine.

"Everyone is used to twenty-four-hour access to me. But that isn't happening anymore. It might take me a few hours to get back to people." The claw pulled at his neck but he took a deep breath, forcing it back. A little. "Again, anyone gives you trouble, you let me know." Apollo looked at his watch again, then up at the apartment complex where his wife lived. "I need to go."

He shut the phone off. All the way off. She'd brought him meals so often. He was finally returning the favor.

Breakfast with Kassie. Kassandra.

He walked up to the door and rang the bell by her apartment. Their penthouse had a doorman. He'd found out her address as soon as she'd moved out. Just to make sure she was okay.

Apollo hadn't expected her to stay in this upscale but small apartment for two years. But then, their huge place felt empty with just him there. Maybe the downsize was good for her.

"Yes?" Her voice sounded sleepy on the other side of the button.

"It's me." He looked at his watch, for the third time. Anxiety was a hell of a gift. It made you work. But you doubted everything else. But he was right. Six-thirty on the dot.

She'd gotten up with him at five during their marriage. Or earlier when deadlines were hitting. He'd assumed she still was.

Assumed.

"Who?"

That stung. "Apollo. It's Apollo, Kass—andra." It had killed him when she asked him to stop calling her Kass. He'd never called her honey, or sweetie or any other partner-type nickname. For him it was Kass.

But if she didn't want that, he'd honor it.

The door buzzed and he hefted the bag his cook had meticulously packed for him over the threshold.

He knocked on her door and Kassandra opened the door wearing a T-shirt and short shorts.

His T-shirt.

"I thought I lost that." His heartbeat exploded in his ears. She was wearing his shirt. *His.*

"Oh." Kass looked down. "Do you want it back?"

"Never."

She looked at the bag then back at him. "What are you doing here, Apollo?"

"Breakfast!" He held up the bag. "I uh… I thought you'd be up." Assuming was a bad idea. Clearly.

"I don't have to be at the office until nine-thirty." She stepped back, covering a yawn.

"I can go." He'd been so certain this was a good idea. Certain she'd be up and about.

Step one in perfect husband mode…and it was wrong. A minor failure…but still failure.

She smiled. "It was a nice gesture." She yawned again. "One that could have waited an hour but come in. I'll start a pot of coffee."

"Oh. Good." She loved coffee. When she was home, their kitchen counter was covered in fancy syrups, and the fridge full of specialty milks. He'd laughed once that she was creating potions more than coffee.

Coffee and Kassandra were synonymous in his mind. He'd spent almost six hours last night poring over every pregnancy blog he could find. Almost all of them assured the reader that women could have small amounts of coffee during their pregnancy.

She moved to the kitchen and he followed. The apartment was small. Not technically. But it could fit into their penthouse at least twice over. Still, she had a full kitchen, dining area, living room and a bedroom.

And it was bright! A blue couch, green chairs

next to a red kitchen table. It was a mix of colors that should seem overwhelming but somehow fit perfectly.

"This is nice." He sat the bag on the counter and started pulling the food out.

"It's mine."

There was something in those two words. A challenge? Pride? A mixture?

"I got to make it colorful."

Got to? He'd have let her do whatever she wanted in their apartment. Though there were expectations when hosting in their wealth classes. Photographic ready…not lived in.

But if this was what she'd wanted, all she had to do was ask. He'd never cared about their living space.

And I never considered that she wanted this.

"I like it." He grinned and held up a container. "I have eggs, salmon and some fruit. It's a little of everything."

She poured a cup of coffee and handed it to him. "The plates are in the cabinet directly in front of you." Then she grabbed a kettle and started to boil the water.

"Please tell me you're having a cup of coffee." He'd barged in on her. Surely, she wasn't just fixing coffee for him.

Of course she is.

"Pregnant. Remember." She ran a hand over her belly. "So it's tea."

"You can have coffee. In small amounts. I read a lot last night. It's perfectly safe for one cup a day."

Kassandra let out a yawn. "Yeah, the problem is that I don't want to have a small amount. I want a giant portion—over and over again." She rubbed her eye then pulled out a diffuser and started measuring a fancy imported loose-leaf tea into it.

"I see." He filled two plates and took them to the kitchen table. Went back for his coffee and then returned to the table.

She let out another yawn before following him.

He really should have planned this better. She'd always been up with him. But that was clearly for him. Not her.

What else was only for him?

Everything.

She slid into her chair and held her teacup between her fingers. "Why are you here, Apollo?"

"I want you to come home." Oof. That was six paragraphs into the topic he planned to discuss.

"No." Kassie lifted the cup to her lips and took a sip. "That all?"

No. He wasn't surprised by the answer, particularly given his clumsy delivery, but there was no hesitation. No gentle letdown. His wife had changed.

Or maybe she was always hiding.

"I am going to be a present father, Kassandra." He started to reach for her arm then pulled back. "I will be there for the baby."

"All right." She shrugged and took another sip of her drink. She wasn't touching her food.

"I mean it. I will be there for our son or daughter." He wanted to bite his tongue. He'd planned out his words. Thought of what he wanted to say and then just barged into the middle of it.

Step two of this plan—failed. This was the definition of crash and burn.

"I want you to be there for them." She looked away from him, toward the kitchen. There was nothing there, so clearly she just didn't want to meet his gaze.

"And for you." There. That was what he'd meant to say. "I want to be there for our son or daughter *and* you."

Kassandra's head whipped toward him, surprise radiating off her gorgeous features. "So early-morning breakfasts?"

"No. Yes. I guess if that's what you want. But I just… I miss you."

Kassandra pulled her bottom lip between her teeth. "Apollo."

"You don't have to answer right now."

"The answer is no." She laid a hand on her belly. "Part of me wants it to be yes. But…" She closed her eyes, and no other words came out.

His entire plan rested on that *but*. He could fix this. Maybe not quickly. If part of her wanted it to be a yes, then there was still a possibility of turning this failure around.

"Kassandra, I messed up. A lot. I get that. Our

marriage was one-sided. I was focused on the office."

"Was." She chuckled. "You say that like it's in the past."

"I worked from the car yesterday."

She raised a brow then took a sip of her tea. "I don't know why you seem so thrilled with that statement."

"All right. Fair. I failed at our marriage. But I can and will fix it."

"Because I'm pregnant." He teacup rattled as she sat it in the saucer.

The claw wrapped around his chest. This was a test. One he needed to pass. "Yes and no. *Yes*, in that you storming into my office yesterday was a wake-up call, and *no*, because I want to fix it."

Kassie looked at him, eyes filled with tears. "And if I don't want to fix it?"

The claw seized him. Clenching. Ripping.

"Then sign the divorce papers, Kass. Kassandra. Sorry. Sign the papers and we will figure out coparenting." He sucked in as deep a breath as the anxiety would allow and then reached for his coffee. "Either way, this is a lovely breakfast, and you should enjoy it. You are eating for two."

She offered a small smile and nodded. "I am eating for two."

They enjoyed the breakfast in relative silence. And he was hyperaware when he left that she hadn't agreed to try again…or told him she was signing the papers.

* * *

Good morning. I am working from home today. Let me know if you want to meet up.

A version of the same text had greeted her every morning since he'd showed up for his unannounced breakfast. She'd been stunned when he first arrived. Stunned, but she hadn't responded.

It wasn't pettiness. She'd promised herself that. She just didn't want to get her hopes up. It was easy to follow up for a day.

Then the next day another message. This time with a little heart on the end. Apollo using an emoji. She'd laughed and almost texted back. Almost.

Yesterday's message contained the same words and with an extra note: hope your day goes well. Kassie ran her hands over the message, hating the excited part of her. Who got excited for such a little thing?

But he'd never texted before. Not first. She'd spent their marriage waiting for him to respond to her.

The texts were nice. Apollo hadn't called but the open greeting was there. As was the not stated undertone of *waiting on you to make your choice*.

Then sign the divorce papers.

Her heart had constricted when he'd issued the words. Not a challenge. Not a threat. Just a simple statement that if she wanted her husband to go away, all she had to do was sign the papers.

Working from home.

How many times during their marriage had she asked, playfully and toward the end with as much heat as her play-nice attitude allowed, for him to work away from his well-appointed office? For him to stay with her. To take a day off.

To see her. To spend time with her. To put her on his agenda.

Now, if the messages were accurate, and she didn't doubt them, then he'd done it for almost a week.

Because I'm pregnant.

He hadn't changed for her. That was what kept her from responding; what held her fingers in place as the silly emojis added up.

A week doesn't equal change.

Kassie cringed. When had her mental voice taken such a hard turn? She was usually the sunny friend. The one whom people came to when they wanted a pick-me-up, not when they were looking to hide a body. A joke Gemma had made a few weeks before her wedding. When Kassie had asked why she would ever need to help hide a body, Gemma and their friend Anna, who was apparently willing to hide a body, no questions asked, had giggled.

She wanted Apollo in their child's life. And that meant he was going to be in her life.

But there was in her life and *in her life*.

Particularly because her phone was silent this morning. She looked at the week's worth of messages. All ending yesterday. Today nothing.

No message. No emoji. No nothing. Why was

it so easy for everyone in Kassie's life to just let her go?

Her father hadn't thought of her since he'd arranged her marriage to a billionaire. The connections that brought him were secure. Even if his relationship with his child was nonexistent. She'd learned long ago that proximity to power was good enough for most people.

Her father had gotten proximity to Apollo and that was enough for his business goals. And her mother was simply happy to have her out of her house. Out of her life.

Particularly since she was no longer playing the role of dutiful wife. The life her parents had crafted her for wasn't hers anymore. They'd cut her off the second she moved in here. Not that it mattered because they hadn't seen her outside social functions in years. But knowing that they didn't want the version of herself that she loved stung.

Apollo didn't want that version, either. He wanted the wife up with him at five. The one who worked her life around his.

What if he doesn't?

She'd changed. Maybe he had, too.

In a week?

She was finally in control of her life and now the past was knocking on her door.

And part of me wants to answer.

The other part of her wanted her to focus on the life she already had. At work she was in control. Mostly. She still answered to Signa and sometimes

Liza, the other senior planner who, in Kassie's opinion, liked to thrust her own opinions into the places they weren't needed.

Still, at the office her life was hers. Her path, her own. She was all too aware that the pregnancy changed that, too. People worked with children. They had good careers but it was different. Her life was unsteady and Apollo hadn't texted.

And she hated how often her gaze went to her phone. To the stupid hope that there was a note. Something to show she wasn't so easily put aside.

She pulled in a ragged breath, forcing herself to steady. She was not showing up to the clinic in tears. Not bawling like a baby because her life wasn't what she'd expected.

Her baby was loved. That was what mattered. And she was going to make damn sure that her little bean never felt like an afterthought.

Pulling into the parking lot of the women's clinic, she let out a sigh. No Bugatti. Not that she'd expected it.

No, she had. That was always the problem. She'd told Apollo about the appointment, and he'd sworn he'd be here. And part of her had believed it.

So that cemented that.

Kassie stepped out of the car as Apollo stepped out of the most boring-looking sedan ever created. "What the hell are you driving?"

He looked back at the car, and she was almost certain that he cringed, but the look was gone before she could be sure.

"No place for a car seat in the Bugatti." He shrugged. "Ready for the doctor?"

"Wait. You're here. And you came in a sedan. Why didn't you text this morning?" Where had that last line come from?

Apollo tilted his head, the ghost of a smile on his lips. "Yes, I came in a sedan. And no, I didn't. I figured we were seeing each other at nine…" His words died off. "A mistake. It won't happen again."

"It's fine. Really, I don't even know why I brought it up. Sorry."

"You do that a lot, you know?" Apollo stepped beside her, the morning sun glinting over his head. Highlighting his beauty. As if he wasn't a man named for the sun god, but the sun god himself. Walking beside her.

And she was just Kassandra. Also named for a mythical woman. One no one wanted to be around. The irony was not lost on her.

"*Fine* is my favorite word." She brushed off his statement and started toward the clinic.

His hand gripped hers and squeezed. "Kass—Kassandra. I meant apologizing for things that are not your fault. *I* didn't text."

She looked at his hand; his fingers twisted through hers. Her throat closed. In another place, another universe, they were entering the clinic together, like this. As partners.

Tasting blood, Kassie realized that she'd bitten the inside of her cheek. Forcing her gaze from their linked hands, she looked into his dark eyes. "Thank you for coming."

He squeezed her hand one more time, then dropped it. "I'm sorry that you doubted I'd be here. You don't have any reason to trust it, but I promise. I am here for this. For whatever you want me to be. Whenever. You just have to ask."

Her heart shook in her chest. She wanted to believe that. Desperately.

"All right. Let's go see the baby."

They stepped through the clinic together. Not holding hands. But together. For right now, that was enough.

"Kassandra Nilson?"

She nodded.

"Wonderful. Doctor Cleson is running ahead of schedule. It's probably the only time that will happen in your pregnancy, but it does mean I can take you and—" The woman looked at Apollo and her eyes widened.

It was a reaction Kassie was used to. No one looked at Apollo and was unmoved.

"Her husband." Apollo nodded, unaware, or at least acting like it, of the woman's besotted expression.

"Of course. You marked single on the intake paperwork. I can take care of that." She pulled her attention away from Apollo and guided them to a room.

After asking basic questions, she stepped out and the room fell into silence.

"Sorry. I marked single..." How was she supposed to finish that sentence? It was true.

And it wasn't.

Apollo gripped her hand, and she didn't pull away.

"I know why you marked it. And stop apologizing." He opened his mouth, but before he could say whatever was next, the doctor walked in.

"Kassandra Nilson, eight weeks along it looks like." The doctor grinned at her, looked at their linked hands. "I assume you're Dad?"

"I am." Apollo looked at Kassie. A look hovering in his eyes that she couldn't quite place.

"Let's take a little look at your bundle and get some baseline measurements." She grabbed the gel from the counter.

Apollo dropped her hand, and Kassie pulled her shirt up and her skirt down a little. They were about to see their child.

The warmed gel hit her belly, and Kassie turned her head toward the doctor. The ultrasound machine was facing the doctor, and Kassie saw the exact moment her face shifted. The clicking of the keys as she added something to the images. The focus on her brow.

The room was nearly silent and yet her ears were pounding with the rushing sounds of her breaths and heartbeat.

She held her hand out and Apollo's was there in an instant.

"What's wrong?" His voice was steady, thank

goodness, because there was no way for her to get any words out.

"Nothing." Dr. Cleson clicked a few more keys on the machine, drawing lines on the ultrasound.

"Your face says differently." Apollo linked his fingers through hers.

A host of reasons she'd found online ran through her mind. There was a reason doctors told you not to go searching. That didn't stop anyone and certainly hadn't stopped her.

The doctor turned the ultrasound around.

Kassie blinked as she looked at the little one squirming on the screen. It looked like little more than a tiny blob but it was her baby.

As was the one next to it.

"Twins." Apollo forced the word out before she could.

"Yes, monozygotic. Or identical." The doctor pointed to the first bean, and the second not far from it. "You can see twin A here and twin B here."

"What does that mean?" Apollo's gaze darted from the screen to her and back again.

He knew what it meant, but she also understood the shock. Twins. Two babies. Identical. So many words bounced in her head.

She let out a chuckle. "It means two car seats." She covered her mouth with her free hand as a nervous giggle threatened to take over. It meant so much more than two car seats, but she couldn't process that right now.

Twins.

She was pregnant with twins.

Apollo's twins.

CHAPTER FOUR

TWINS.

The word was dancing in his brain as they stepped out of the clinic. Everything had changed and yet the world moved on without a blink.

The sun was shining. The wind blowing just a little. The day was gorgeous.

So was the woman standing next to him blinking in the sunlight.

"Your sunglasses are on top of your head, sweetie." The endearment slipped out. He'd never called her anything other than Kassie or Kass. But she'd asked him not to do that and he was doing his best to honor that.

Still, it felt weird on his tongue. Not wrong, but not right, either.

Kassie reached her hand up, touching the glasses, and then sliding them down. "Is it too early to blame baby brain?" She let out a giggle that sounded a little panicky. "Or because I have two babies growing, do I get to do everything earlier? That almost seems fair. Right? I mean…there are two." Her hand started toward her face.

He grabbed it. It was a reaction she'd done when they'd first started dating. She was taught to say nothing. And when her brain started wandering, she had a habit of pulling her hand over her mouth. She'd stopped it, but apparently the habit had returned.

She hadn't realized it then. He doubted she realized it now. But it was a Kass-ism, as he'd once mentally called it, ingrained by her parents. Be seen, never heard.

He hated it. Apollo wanted all of her words. All of her thoughts.

"Breathe." He gripped both her hands. "Breathe." He took a deep breath and let it out, repeated it until she started to follow his cues.

"Sorry."

"One." He kissed her lips. The action caught her off guard. Him, too. But she didn't pull away.

"One?" She shook her head. "No. There are most definitely two."

"Yes, there are. But that one is counting the sorry. I will add to it, each time you say it."

"Sorry." She snapped her mouth closed.

"Two." He pressed his lips to her forehead. "Why don't we go get some lunch. You are officially eating for three."

"Three."

He pulled her close, enjoying the feel of holding her a little too much. "Three."

Her head lay against his shoulder for a few minutes. There was no way he was breaking this connection first.

"Don't you have to work?" She uttered the words then stepped back.

"I have a free morning and early afternoon. I can adjust the few things I have on my calendar, too." Then stay up late tonight seeing to anything that needed finishing.

He hated the suspicious look in her eyes. Had he really not been around that much?

Yes.

His brain saw no reason to lie to him. "I am here. I meant that."

"So you've worked from home this week?"

"Not the whole week." He saw the flick of something pass along her face. "But most days. I had to go in to talk a client out of a poor economic decision. He said he'd only take my advice in person."

Apollo had tried to work through a few things through email. But the client had insisted that his astrologer told him that the stock was a surefire bet. That Venus and Mars were in alignment. That he was certain this was the real deal.

It absolutely was not.

"Ever think of dropping the client?"

"If they decide to take the advice of their astrologer on stocks, yeah. Maybe." He wrapped an arm around her shoulder, grateful when she didn't pull away. "Lunch? I'll drive."

"All right." She let him guide her to the sedan. Technically, it was a Porsche. But it did not look like a sports car. Or it did. It just didn't look like the sports cars he liked to drive. But he hadn't lied; there was no place for a car seat in the Bugatti. So he needed something with a backseat.

He slid into the driver's seat.

"Astrologer? You're really competing with an astrologer giving economic advice?" Kassie's hands were tight in her lap.

He suspected this was a safe conversation. And that was what she needed as she processed the doctor's appointment. Their lives had shifted with the pregnancy, but she'd had weeks to adjust to the idea.

With twins, everything was very different, again.

"Yeah. I don't personally believe in it, but I am not against people looking to the stars or anything else that gives them support. However, this was a super-bad idea."

"Again, you could drop them."

"They're my parents' friend." Not that his parents were speaking to him these days, but he still invested most of their friends' money. An irony not lost on him.

What would they do when they heard Kassie was pregnant? His parents had fought for the two of them to marry. His father made millions in real estate. It opened many doors but not those locked by generational wealth. So they'd set their sights on the aristocracy. A family with the right ties but not as many business ties.

Kassie's family was perfect. Her father was only too happy to have a billionaire for a son-in-law.

They'd never disclosed to either family that they'd met at a writers' group weeks before and actually gone on a few dates. A few wonderful dates. The happiest time in his life.

The last thing his mother had called him was a failure.

He'd not known what to say. He hated how they reacted but he was the man he was because of them. That counted for the little bit of respect he gave when mutual friends asked after them.

They'd probably reach out when they heard Kassie was carrying his child. Part of him, the child who'd never gotten the affection he wanted, was desperate for that call. That part was far larger than he wanted to admit.

"Where to for lunch?" Kassie's soft tone broke his mental wanderings.

"I was heading to Kloni. You love their lunch sandwiches." Her nose scrunched, but she nodded her head.

"Kass." The name slipped out. "You clearly don't want to go there."

She whipped her head toward him. He'd earned that. The name she'd asked him not to say had just popped out. "It's fine. I don't mind."

He'd expected an argument. She was simply giving him what she thought he wanted.

"Let me guess. I like the sandwiches and you've

just gone along with it." He hated how clearly that was the case.

She shrugged. "They're fine."

"I am going to start counting fines next." Apollo took a deep breath. "Where am I going, Kassandra?"

"I like Il Café. They have these giant salads. And they do not skimp on the dressing." She rubbed a hand over her belly. "But seriously, I don't mind Kloni."

"*And I don't mind* Il Café." The truth was that he was not a fan of salads. Particularly big ones. He liked his protein from meat. But his wife was going to get what she wanted this time.

"All right. If you're sure." She relaxed a little. A tiny win. But one he was going to celebrate.

"Very."

Her stomach rumbled. Even though she'd eaten all her salad and not a small amount of Apollo's, too. He'd said he wasn't that hungry, but Kassie knew it was simply that he wasn't a huge fan of the fare at Il Café.

But he'd come. For her.

Because I'm pregnant.

She couldn't forget that. He wasn't here for her. No one was ever here for Kassie. She had to make her own way in this life.

"Any interest in dessert? Anna's bakery is just around the corner." She wasn't sure why she was prolonging this outing.

I like having his time. I'm soaking it in. I don't want to let it go.

Because it won't last.

Her heart was more than happy to provide the reason. And her brain the caution.

"I could go for a cookie." Apollo stood and moved to pull her chair out for her.

She looked at her watch.

"Do you have somewhere to be?" His voice was low as he leaned toward her.

"It's one." He'd told her that he'd rearrange his schedule this afternoon. But she didn't really think he'd meant it.

"Okay." He shrugged. "I'm not keeping track of time, Kassandra."

Kassandra. He'd listened to her. Though he'd slipped up once. And she wanted him to slip again. Craved it. But she'd demanded the formality, and she wasn't going to step back. Not now.

"Your meetings." Might as well throw it out.

"You want dessert." He opened the door of the bistro and led them out to his car. "Right? You brought it up. If you've changed your mind, that is fine. Though I will be finding a cookie or something else shortly."

She had brought it up. And she did want a treat.

"I am not leaving until you want me to. Period." His dark gaze held hers. The truth was rooted there. He wasn't plotting how quickly to get away and back to the mountains of paperwork and responsibilities his company demanded.

A weight lifted off her chest. She pursed her lips to keep the bright smile from forming. This was just a start.

Because of the twins.

They aren't here.

Yet.

Why was her brain constantly at odds with her heart? Because it was trying to protect her.

"Kassandra? Am I driving to the bakery or to the clinic so you can grab your car? I want to be clear there is no wrong answer here and no need for an apology either way." He opened the door of the car and waited for her to slip in, then gently closed it.

When he took his seat, she laid a hand over his. His gaze rooted to their joined hands. He'd taken her hand several times today, but this was the first time she'd initiated the contact—outside of when she was terrified at the clinic. But that didn't really count.

"Bakery."

He started to lean toward her and, for a second, she thought he might kiss her, but he pulled back. Which was good. His lips had brushed hers twice today. Accidental slips into the past.

Today was weird. An anomaly. They were both reacting. The spell wouldn't last but she was clinging to every bit of magic she could.

They pulled up outside the bakery, and she slid out before he got to her door. "I know Gemma loves the iced cookies, but I am fond of the *kladdkakas*."

The chocolate cake balls were her favorite. And Anna made a mint one that was simply to die for.

"*Kladdkakas?*" He tilted his head. "Since when?"

"Since always. Chocolate everything. You prefer vanilla and strawberry but for me, it's chocolate." She saw him stiffen and she wasn't exactly sure the reason. "You don't have to worry. Anna has several vanilla options. Probably not a lot of strawberries. Given that it's past their growing season. Though just past, so who knows, maybe she still has some." She crossed her fingers and laughed, hoping to wipe the frown off his face.

"I'm not worried about dessert, Kassandra." The words were formal and somehow, even though she'd asked for the formal name, hearing it tacked onto the sentence sent a shiver down her throat. She opened her mouth to apologize but snapped it shut. She wasn't sure what she'd done wrong, but she didn't want another sorry on the counter.

She pulled open the door and let out a sigh as the sugary scents hit her.

"Coming!"

Kassie froze. That wasn't Anna's voice or her bakery assistant. And based on the panic setting into Apollo's face, he also recognized Gemma's voice.

Her friend exited the back, blinked twice then smiled. "Kassandra. Apollo." Gemma's smile wasn't quite forced, but it was tight.

"You aren't at Pairably?" The tech company

Gemma ran was booming. The dating app she'd created was the hottest thing in the upper class.

She'd tried it once. And matched with Arthur. The moment had made her laugh…and then cry because she'd missed Apollo so much. She'd ditched the dating app, and any plan for dating after that.

Gemma blushed. "Don't tell Arthur. We tried to make the cookies I love so much. It was a disaster, many times, actually. Anna is teaching me. She ran to the store to get some vanilla and I told her I could run the register for her since Elin's son isn't feeling well.

"What brings you *two* in?" The emphasis on two was not subtle.

"I'm pregnant. With twins. Apollo's." She knew her husband's head had snapped toward her. She could hardly blame him. Kassandra hadn't planned to say anything. Hell, she wasn't quite sure why she had. But the announcement was out.

"What?" Gemma blinked a few times.

Kassie placed a hand over her belly. "Yeah. Twins. Apollo's." That didn't really need repeating, but her brain seemed stuck. "Eight weeks, plus a few days. We saw the images this morning. Two little beans."

Gemma came around the bakery counter. "All right. How are you feeling? Am I saying congratulations, or helping you murder him? Anna is in either way."

"I'm standing right here." Apollo's words were

light, or as light as possible with his sister-in-law threatening to murder him.

Kassie let out a little laugh. "Happy. And terrified. And excited and scared out of my mind."

Gemma pulled her into her arms.

She looked over Gemma's shoulder. Apollo was looking at her. His gaze so soft. It would be far too easy to slip into the Kassie she'd been. She was going to have to find a way to keep her guard up.

"I'm going to be an aunt." Gemma tightened her grip.

Before she let go, the bell over the door rang, and Kassie saw Anna walk through. "Why is the ex here? Are we burying him?"

"Seriously, should I be concerned that my sister-in-law and my *wife's* friend are both fine with her leading me in here to my demise?"

His emphasis on the word *wife* hit her straight in the heart. How many times had she wanted to hear him claim her? How many events had she stood alone at, hoping, and knowing that she was by herself?

Anna raised a brow as she walked up to Gemma and her. "Are we?"

Apollo let out a strangled sound.

"No." Kassandra giggled.

"Thank you." Apollo gave her a little grin. She wasn't sure if that was because he was happy that she'd cleared him or to pacify Anna. Either way, she was fine with it.

"I'm pregnant." She'd already told Gemma, and

she knew Anna wouldn't share it further. "With twins."

"His," Anna said as her eyes cut to Apollo, "I assume."

"Yes." Her cheeks heated. "We came to get a dessert after lunch. We saw the OB this morning at the women's clinic. My brain is still not quite registering that I'm pregnant."

"Did you want dessert?" Anna headed behind the counter and set her bags down, tied her apron then washed her hands before turning back around.

"I mean, we wanted dessert." She looked to Apollo. "Right?"

Apollo nodded to her then met Anna's gaze head-on. "I want what Kassandra wants."

"Really?" Anna smiled a grin that Kassandra knew had nothing nice in it. "Then what is it that Kassandra always wants from my bakery?"

"A *kladdkaka*." Apollo crossed his arms.

Anna chuckled. "Cute. What *kladdkaka*?" She gestured toward the counter display where six different versions sat.

"Apollo—"

He held up a hand and Kassie held her tongue. "I got this."

Except he didn't. She'd mentioned the *kladdkaka*. Mentioned loving chocolate but there was one *kladdkaka* that she always got here. One that was far from the bestseller. In fact, Anna didn't even make it every day but the mint *kladdkaka* was there. As was a cinnamon, double chocolate, white chocolate, one with a berry sauce and the traditional chocolate one.

A one in six shot.

"Apollo."

He waved a hand—again. "I said I got this." There was a hint of worry in his tone. "The double chocolate."

"Wrong." Anna let out a truly exasperated sigh.

"Enough. I know this isn't what you expected. It isn't what I expected, either, but Apollo is the father of my children, and we are trying to make this work."

His head popped toward her. "We are?"

"Why is he asking that like it's a question?" Anna raised her brow.

Gemma cleared her throat. "I know your ex-fiancé was an ass, Anna, but this is Kassandra's life."

Anna pursed her lips but finally nodded. "Fine."

"Truce?" Apollo reached his hand across the counter, but Anna rolled her eyes.

"I just washed my hands, man. Good grief, your bloke is thick." Anna reached into the counter and pulled out the biggest mint *kladdkaka*. "This is the answer. Mint. Mint and chocolate. You guys were married for not a small amount of time. She never gets anything else."

Anna took a deep breath then trained her gaze on Apollo. "If you hurt her again, it will not be jokes about me hiding your body."

"Duly noted."

"He wants a strawberry cookie, Anna." Kassandra stepped beside Apollo and ran the back of her hand against his.

He returned the motion. So small, but it grounded her.

"Is she right?" Anna looked from her to Apollo. The knowledge already clear in her gaze.

"Yes."

Anna rolled her eyes and pulled the cookie out, setting it in the box beside hers. "On the house." Her friend's bright blue eyes trained on hers, softening. "As a congrats."

"Thank you, Anna." She took the box.

"I meant it earlier. Don't tell Arthur that I was here. I want it to be a surprise." Gemma gave her a quick squeeze.

Anna nodded her head toward them. "When it's time for the baby shower, I get to make the cake."

"Of course." Kassandra smiled and ran her free hand over her belly. "I wouldn't have it any other way."

She turned to Apollo. "Ready?"

He looked at Gemma and Anna one more time, then nodded. "Absolutely."

They went out to the little table sitting beside the door. She slid into a chair and pulled out her treat and the takeaway fork. She took one bite, closing her eyes and reveling in the hint of mint with the delicious chocolate.

"Good?"

"Yes." She opened her eyes. "I'm sorry. Anna and Gemma—"

"Three." Apollo reached over and gripped her hand. "No need to apologize. And Anna and Gemma are protective. As they should be. Though Anna is a little scary."

"Honestly, Anna is a softie. Mostly." She grinned and looked into the bakery, where both her friends were doing odd jobs.

Odd jobs that let them keep an eye on the table Apollo and Kassie were sitting at.

She waved and both women turned quickly. "Not stealthy at all. I didn't mean to tell them I was pregnant. It just popped out."

Apollo took a bite of his cookie and let out a moan. Once upon a time, that moan would turn her insides inside out. Technically, it still did, but she wasn't going to act on that.

"Anna is scary as hell, but an excellent baker."

Kassie grinned. "She is."

Apollo reached his hand over, placing it over hers. "But you get to tell people whatever. I am here for the ride. All right?"

She waited a moment. Waited to see if he'd mention that she'd said they were trying to work it out. It had popped out. He'd reacted in the moment but then Anna had commanded the room again.

"Kassandra?" He held up the cookie. "Are you eyeing my cookie? 'Cause I'll share but I will complain a little."

They weren't the words she wanted but she brushed the twinge of hurt away. "No. You can keep your cookie, because I'm not sharing my *kladdkaka*."

CHAPTER FIVE

APOLLO WOKE AND immediately sent a text to Kassandra. She likely wouldn't see it for at least another hour, but he wanted her to know he was thinking of her.

Needed her to know.

Yesterday's visit to the bakery had been more than eye opening. How could he not have known her love for chocolate and mint? Her favorite treat. A staple, if her friend's not-so-subtle threats were any indication. It was such a simple thing.

A simple thing I didn't know.

He yawned but swung his legs out from his bed. The bed that used to be his and Kassie's. He looked over at the pillow her head should be resting on.

His phone buzzed. He looked at it and ran his fingers over the words.

Hope you slept well. K

Four words.

A response.

He let out a sigh. He could right this path. Be a

good husband and father. No. Be an excellent husband and father. The best.

His phone buzzed again, this time with a notification that someone was asking for entrance.

Kassie? He stood and started walking toward the door, then answered the buzzer. "Good morning."

"Morning. You sound happy." Arthur's cool tone on the other end surprised him. He shouldn't have expected Kassie. But his heart couldn't help but hope.

He buzzed his brother up and let him in.

"Are you just getting up?"

Apollo titled his head. "I think the appropriate greeting is *good morning*."

"I already said that." Arthur passed him a cup. "Black."

"Thanks." Apollo took a deep sip. "Not that I'm not happy to see you—"

"But you aren't happy to see me? Is that because my wife and her best friend threatened to bury you yesterday?" Arthur walked down the hallway. "This place is boring as hell, man."

"Yeah, I know. I didn't say I wasn't happy to see you. But Gemma and Anna are a little scary." Apollo followed his brother. Whatever this morning was, it clearly wasn't a have-coffee-in-the-entryway-of-his-penthouse type of conversation. "Why are you here?"

"I hear I'm going to be an uncle. Twins." Arthur lifted the coffee to his lips but didn't sit on the couch.

Apollo shrugged. “Are you upset because I’m giving Mom and Dad the first grandchildren?”

Where had that come from?

His parents wanted grandchildren. They’d started pestering him and Kass the moment they got married. But given that they hadn’t talked to him since she’d vacated the premises…

“I worry that you started with that.” Arthur shook his head. “I have no contact with our parents. When Gemma and I decide to have children, you are the only family member that will know. On either side.”

Apollo watched his brother’s reaction. It was one thing not to invite them to the wedding. He and Arthur had craved that attention. Battled for it. Lost themselves in some ways to it.

Arthur had cut them off. Apollo was cut off. The distinction burned. Maybe if he’d made the choice a tiny piece of his soul wouldn’t yearn to hear his mother call him *son* with the soft tone she’d use when she was happy.

The claw creeped up his neck at the memory of his mother turning away from the kiss he’d dropped on her cheek whenever he saw her…before. He didn’t particularly enjoy depositing a kiss there, but it was a family expectation.

One he somehow missed.

Now he achieved for himself. But the shine he’d always felt was dulled. Once he had Kassie back, when his life was fully on track, every part successful, the contentment would come.

It had to.

"Kassie is great. I didn't really get to know her while you two were married." Arthur's dark gaze held his as he raised the cup to his lips.

"We're still married." Apollo squeezed the cup of coffee, glaring at the top as it flew off.

"Careful." Arthur bent down, retrieving the lid. "You wouldn't want to stain the boring Persian rug." He handed the lid back to his brother.

"Why are you here?" Apollo put the lid back on. "Our relationship isn't the drop-in-before-work-starts kind."

Arthur let out a sigh. "It could be."

Could it? Was it possible given the distance between them?

"But I'm here for Kassandra. Because Gemma is worried about her. And when my wife is worried, I worry." There was a hint of judgment there. A pointed reminder that Arthur knew his bride.

Or perhaps the dig was simply in Apollo's mind. Either way, it didn't change the outcome.

"I am aware that I wasn't the best husband. I plan to fix that. Be the best. Perfect."

"Perfect husband or father?"

"Both." Why was that so hard to believe? He'd achieved every goal he'd set for himself. And more. "I've rearranged things. Moved work around. I can and will make this work, Arthur."

His brother tilted his head. "For Kassandra? Or for you?" He held up a hand. "Don't answer. It's not for me. But *you* need to know. And if it isn't for her, then let her go."

"I can make her happy." Apollo didn't know what else to say. Thankfully, Arthur didn't seem to need or want anything else.

"I hope that is the case. I really do. I want you happy. I want Kassandra happy, too." He looked at his watch. "I've done my husbandly duty here and I promised Gemma *smörgås*. She loves cod paste. I know others love it. But it isn't my thing." He hesitated for a moment, looking like he wanted to say something else, but the words weren't coming.

Either way, he walked out, leaving Apollo unsure of exactly what had happened.

His phone buzzed and he read the message and grinned.

Hungry. Like really hungry. I am blaming the twins. Want to grab breakfast? We can go to Vassa.

He didn't hesitate to respond in the affirmative and tell her he'd pick her up in thirty minutes. The place she mentioned was one of the most upscale restaurants in Stockholm.

A place that didn't open until six and definitely didn't serve breakfast.

That did not mean Kassie wasn't getting exactly what she wanted. He dialed a number, offered an obscene amount of money, but got his confirmation that the chef would be there as soon as he was walking out the door.

What Kassie wanted, Kassie got.

* * *

Kassie saw the empty parking lot and immediately hit the palm of her hand against her forehead. “Vassa doesn’t serve breakfast. How did I not remember that? Or rather, why would I think they would?”

Apollo pulled her hand from her forehead, his thumb running along the base of her wrist for a second. Not even a second. A microsecond that sent heat straight to her core.

Focus.

“It’s open.” He pulled the Porsche sedan into the very empty parking lot.

“I hate to point this out, but umm…no, it isn’t.” Kassie gestured toward the empty lot as she leaned her head back. The luxury sedan wasn’t what Apollo typically drove but it was comfy. “This place, when open, is always packed.”

Apollo lifted her hand and for a second, she thought he might kiss her fingers. Instead, he held it for a moment before letting it go. “Do you trust me?”

She wanted to. Desperately. She’d texted this morning. Unsure what to say. Rambling…in text. And he’d answered right away. And shown up exactly thirty minutes later. Just like he said he would.

That was lovely. Perfect. But the word *yes* wouldn’t drop from her lips.

“Sorry.” The word slipped out, and she muttered, “Four.”

Apollo chuckled but the sound was clearly

forced. "If you count then it makes my job easier. But really, the hesitation is all right. No need for an apology, Kassandra. I haven't earned your trust. But I will."

The certainty in his words should make her happy. But there was a hint of something in his gaze. The same hint she saw when he was acquiring a business, or seeking an accolade. She was not an accolade.

I am reading too much into this.

But what if she wasn't? He'd ignored her…until she was pregnant. Her family had ignored her growing up, unless she was doing something they could use to advance their place in society.

But she was the one who wanted a family. Apollo was open to the idea but never focused on it. Maybe this was for her.

Maybe.

Her stomach rumbled, breaking the car's uncomfortable tension.

"I called the owner. And the chef. I made sure it's open—for us." He slid from the car and was at her door before she could fully process the words.

"Open? Seriously?" He'd known it wasn't open when she texted. Known it was a mistake. Instead of suggesting a new place, he'd made this happen.

For her.

"I made an offer the chef and owners couldn't refuse." He took her hand and helped her from the Porsche. Not that she needed help, though in a few months, even the higher car would be difficult for her to manage.

An offer.

In other words, he'd paid an obscene amount of money to make sure the chef was here with staff. Marriage to one of the most successful men in Sweden—hell, in Europe—was supposed to have perks. She just wasn't used to getting the perk.

"Thank you. Are you going to judge me if I order a steak? I know that it's not even eight yet, but I'm so hungry." She ran a hand along her belly. This morning she'd noticed a tiny bump.

Well, tiny was not quite right. Her pants were more than a little tight. Her dresses, too. It didn't seem possible. Seven months seemed so far away. But also so close.

Everything was changing. But right now, she couldn't focus on the upheaval. Maybe with a full belly she could put more words to the feeling.

Apollo wrapped an arm around her shoulder then dropped it as they started toward the entrance.

She grabbed his arm and put it back. The hunger, and even the craving for meat, she could lay at the feet of the babies. The need for connection with him? That was all her.

He didn't comment on it. Apollo also didn't stop the connection when they reached the door; he slid his hand to her lower back.

She sensed his hesitation. The light touch, the wait for her to pull away. Kassie should. Her brain knew it, but right now her heart was in control of her motions, and it was not going to let her pull away.

They reached the table, ordered, and Apollo asked for some rolls.

"Are you wanting rolls?" Kassie grinned. "I know you love bread but that isn't a normal thing to order here." She giggled and shook her head. "Though I guess it isn't normal to be here for breakfast at all. Thank you."

It meant more than he knew that he'd made this happen.

"I will never turn bread down, but they're for you. If your stomach keeps making noises, the owner might think I've kept you locked away for ages with no food."

She shook her head. "Apollo—" The rolls were deposited before she could finish, and her stomach immediately launched into a chorus of rumbles.

Apollo reached for one, passing it to her. "I think the babies are hungry."

Babies.

She took the roll and tried to ignore the twinge in her throat. He was right. She was so hungry because she was pregnant. Other women dealt with horrid morning sickness. She didn't even have a hint. She was lucky.

Apollo was here for her *because of the babies.*

Heat burned in her chest. She tore off a hunk of bread and dropped it into her mouth. He was here. For her. He'd called in a favor *for* her.

A favor I wouldn't need if I wasn't pregnant.

"Do you still write?" Apollo leaned over, snatching a roll, and let out a soft sigh when he ate a piece.

"Not lately." She shrugged. Once upon a time, she'd pretended the mystery author she'd met at that writing group was the real Apollo. The one who felt like a soul mate. A way out of the life she'd been raised in.

Only for reality to set in…hard.

"Why aren't you writing?" Apollo took another bite of bread.

"Life." She let out an uncomfortable sound. She hadn't gone back to the writers' group since the separation. Partly because she didn't want to answer questions, though she doubted anyone would have pressed, but mostly because her work was so dreary post-separation.

She didn't want to read it, let alone share it.

Now life was better. But the words didn't come. Unlike for him, writing was her fun pursuit. For him, it had always felt like a passion. A passion he refused to let himself fully enjoy. Like there was something shameful in the pursuit.

For her, passion was working at the wedding planning office. She loved the hustle. The closeness to love. Though a bride had asked her yesterday to move her wedding to another planner.

It was a request she'd probably needed to honor anyway, given her due date. But the fact that the bride had acted upset, put off, as if Kassie's life choices were a personal problem for *her*, rubbed her the wrong way. Not that she'd shown it.

She'd kept a perfect smile on. Said she understood. Pretended it didn't sting. It would have just been a regular life story. Except Signa had sided with the bride.

She'd told Kassie that the expectation when the couple booked was broken. *Broken.*

Signa reiterated at least three times that it wasn't Kassie's fault, but that didn't change the bride's needs. Kassie understood, but the anger and frustration from the bride, and subtle discontent of Signa, stung.

And she hated that it stung. She was pregnant. She'd always wanted to be a mom. It shouldn't bother her.

None of those feelings made for great poetry. Or maybe they did; she just didn't want to write those words. Which meant she didn't want to talk about the empty pages in her writing journal.

With the writers' group…or her husband.

"Miss your office at home? Maybe it would help to be in the space." His face brightened and she hated popping that balloon.

"No. I don't miss the penthouse." She paused, then pressed forward. He'd asked her to come home. A request she'd immediately disregarded. For a host of reasons. But there was one more. "I don't miss the penthouse. I hated it when I left. It felt like a tomb."

Apollo pursed his lips. "A tomb. Poetic. And heartbreaking."

Like all of her poetry in the past few years. "Sorry."

He grabbed her hand, squeezing. "Five." Before he could say anything else, their breakfast, that was much more like dinner, arrived.

They ate in silence.

As they were leaving, Apollo slipped his hand around her waist. "You are too talented not to write. If you figure out what you need to bring back the spark, let me know. I'll make it happen."

She laid her head against his shoulder for just a moment, a moment that she wanted to snapshot and carry with her. "I enjoy writing, but not writing doesn't bother me like it does you."

"You are talented."

It was unnecessary but nice to hear. "I appreciate the vote of confidence." She put a finger over his lips before he could argue. "You can't cure my writer's block, Apollo."

"I can try."

"I don't need to be fixed." She was who she wanted to be. That was enough for now.

He pressed his lips to the top of her head. For a second, she considered raising her head. Running her lips along his. Let herself live in this time, in this second, where it felt like perfection might be possible.

But she'd grown comfortable in that dream once. And waking had nearly killed her. She couldn't fall into it again.

CHAPTER SIX

On my way.

THE TEXT WAS her nightmare. And her biggest dream.

Apollo was on his way. They were headed to dinner. Dinner at her favorite steakhouse. The twins seemed to only want red meat. Something that, before this pregnancy, she'd eaten rarely.

Her belly twisted, like she hadn't eaten a snack an hour ago. She was grateful that she didn't have horrid morning sickness. But her body was not her own right now. There were times when she felt like she was just a vessel for the twins' cravings.

That did not mean she didn't want dinner tonight. A dinner Apollo had planned. Planned and showed up for. He was keeping his promise to be present.

For the babies.

Kassie swallowed the pain that thought brought up. She wished there were a way to put her worries to rest. Wished there were some way to believe that Apollo was here for her.

But I reached out first.

That was the kicker. She'd had to reach out. Tell him about his children. But she'd broken her promise.

And I don't think he'd ever reach out to me.

That was the worry she couldn't put away. He didn't want her for herself. Not really.

And yet, her heart was reverting. Or rather, opening back up. She'd loved him when she married him. Loved him when she left him. Loved him when he stepped back into her life.

He was the one for her but she refused to lose herself to the life she'd had before. She wouldn't be a shadow in her own home again.

Tonight was just another meal.

They were going to dinner. Dinner. Something they'd done so many times since their early-morning breakfast.

Not a date. He hadn't said that it was. He never said it was.

And I never ask.

Because asking might put whatever was happening the past two weeks into some weird perspective. He was here.

Whenever she texted, she got an immediate answer. They'd had takeaway at her place. Mostly because she still wasn't ready to enter the penthouse.

A tomb. She'd uttered the word without thinking. It was an uncomfortable truth. Still, it was his home. Maybe she should go for him. But the hurt that place represented was too much. Soon, but not tonight.

Tonight was just supposed to be dinner. Except he'd said he had a surprise for her. A surprise he'd refused to give any insight into. A surprise that had filled her head for the past two days.

She was thrilled. No one gave her surprises. She'd planned more than one surprise engagement with a partner who wanted an over-the-top way to pop the question. It was a service few exercised at her office, but whenever the service was booked, it was always exhilarating.

Her own surprise. She was more than a little scared about what all of this meant. And terrified that it didn't mean anything.

Not that it mattered right now. Right now, she needed to get ready. She still hadn't figured out what she was wearing. Or rather, she'd tried and failed to figure it out.

Because nothing fits!

"Ugh!" She pulled up the sixth pair of pants she'd tried on and once again, the button refused to close. She was only ten weeks. Ten weeks and already out of her clothes. She'd read the twin blogs. Knew other women who'd started showing with twins at eight weeks. And still, somehow, she hadn't expected that she would show this soon.

How did nothing in here fit?

Well, not nothing. She had leggings and sweatpants. Even her dresses with loose waists were too tight to be comfortable for long. More than one bride this week had congratulated her, then paused, clearly wondering if they'd guessed wrong.

There was a knock at her door and she burst into tears. Great. The last thing she wanted was to cry. But her body—and her emotions—were no longer her own. Her body belonged to the twins.

Time was up and she was no closer to being ready than she had been thirty minutes ago when his text popped in.

Apollo was here. And she was standing in her bedroom in pants that didn't fit. Hormones dancing around and a stomach that wanted food. Now!

Another knock. She needed to move, but her feet were rooted to the floor. Her gaze staring at the latest pair of pants that didn't fit.

"Kassandra!" There was panic in his voice. The good news was she'd left the door unlocked. The bad news… It probably created more panic since she hadn't answered.

Another strike against her breaking emotions but she still couldn't move.

"Back here." She didn't try to hide the despair in her voice. What was the point? There was no hiding the open pants. The tear-streaked cheeks. Or the runny mascara.

Good thing this probably wasn't a date.

"What's wrong?" The words were out before he hit the door of her room. He paused at the threshold, no doubt stunned by the spectacle before him.

"Kassie, what's wrong?"

"Sorry I'm not ready. And I swear, if you say twenty-seven I will throw you out of my apartment, because I am sorry that I'm not ready. Sorry that none of my pants fit. Sorry that my body feels alien. Sorry that my stomach is so grumbly I can barely think. Sorry that the only thing we seem to have eaten in the past week is some form of red meat." She let out another sob.

She was getting better at catching the sorries. Not great, but better. But if he added those to her standing total of twenty-six she was going to lose the tiny thread of sanity she was not truly holding on to.

He pulled out his phone, typed something. Probably ordering his assistant to cancel their reservation. That made sense. Wasn't like she could go out like this anyway.

"I was really looking forward to dinner." She rubbed the back of her hand across her cheek. No need to worry about makeup tonight.

"We will still get dinner."

"Apollo!" She threw her hands up in the air. "I cannot wear sweatpants to the fanciest place in Stockholm. Even if they didn't have a dress code, which they very much do, I just can't."

She pulled the pants off, then realized that she was standing in the room in just her panties. Panties that were also stretched to the brink. What the hell, they were married. Sort of. And he'd knocked her up wearing far less than this.

He started toward her, and she held up a hand. "If you are about to tell me to take a deep breath, I swear, I might just murder you."

She hiccupped as he froze. "Sorry. That one

can count." She slid down the edge of her bed and pulled her knees to her chest. Or pulled them to her chest as much as she still could.

Her body really did have an alien feel to it.

Apollo's heat flooded her as he slid down to the floor with her. "I am not counting any of those. I'm sorry that your body is out of your control."

"How terrible do I sound?" Her mother had screamed at her so often that her body was never the same after Kassie. Never the same after the daughter she didn't want.

She'd sworn she'd never be her mother. Sworn when she had children she'd be more. Happy. Content. A mother who showed them love. That wanted them. And yet, here she was sobbing because her pants no longer closed.

Who was she?

She laid her hands on her knees. She could hold the position for a moment or two before it became uncomfortable. Mentally, she laughed at herself. Before it became *too* uncomfortable. Because the last word she'd use right now was *comfortable*.

"You do not sound terrible." His finger brushed a piece of hair from her cheek. The touch was soft. Comforting.

"Liar." She offered what she knew was a watery smile. But she appreciated his statement. "I'm pregnant."

He leaned in. "I know."

The giggle escaped. "You are responsible for this, if you think about it. All of this is your fault."

"It is."

She rolled her eyes. "Please, Apollo. You're not actually responsible. At least not any more than I am. I just hate that I didn't plan better. I should have started looking for maternity clothes the first time I closed my pants with a ponytail holder." That was only a few days ago, but she'd figured she had more time.

The back of his hand stroked her leg. "This is a lot, Kassie. Sorry, Kassandra."

"I'm sitting on the bedroom floor in panties that are too small, carrying *your* twins. I think you can call me Kassie." She'd wanted to hear the name off his lips for more than a week now. Honestly, she'd hated asking him to stop. It was her preferred name, and only he called her that.

"Kassie." He laid his head against hers. Her name sounded like a prayer on his lips. "Can we order takeaway? If you want to go, I will make a call, we'll use the back entrance and have a private room. I can make that happen. I will also make sure that not a single thing is said about you arriving in sweatpants."

She turned her head, her lips brushing his. There was no heat in the moment, just a sweet comfort of hearing exactly what she needed repeated. "Thank you. Takeaway sounds great."

His dark gaze held hers, a look she couldn't quite interpret in it. "All right, but we still have to leave your apartment." He pulled her into his arms. "No one will see the sweatpants, promise. But if you'll trust me, I will fix all of this."

She saw his throat bob. Trust. He'd asked that two weeks ago and she'd hesitated. She still wasn't fully there but she wanted to know what the surprise was. The surprise her outburst here was undoubtedly putting a damper on. "You promise no one will see me?"

"I swear it." Apollo dipped his head, his lips caressing hers.

A shift was happening. Hope was blooming no matter how much she pushed it down. Her brain refused to put up walls. They'd crashed down sometime between breakfast at Vassa and today. They were rock solid once.

No. Where Apollo was concerned, I've never really had walls.

Apollo feared he'd blink and Kassie would evaporate. He'd gotten her into the limo and immediately given his driver new instructions then put the divider up. She wanted privacy and he was giving her that.

"Where are we going?" Her head was against his shoulder. She'd kissed him. Light brushes of her lips. And she hadn't pulled away when he'd done the same.

There was a magic here that he dared not break. He wasn't sure how long it would last. But he wasn't wasting a second.

"I told you. Surprise." He pressed his lips to

the top of her head. His arm tightened around her shoulder. She still hesitated when he mentioned trusting him, which made sense.

But she'd trust him for this. A giant step toward finally righting this ship.

"Surprise." Kassie let out a little sound.

"What does that sound mean?" His fingers ran along the bare skin on the edge of the T-shirt she was wearing. The T-shirt she'd worn the day he shocked her with breakfast.

The one she used to wear around their penthouse. His shirt.

"It *means*—" she looked at him, her jade eyes flashing with humor and a little uncertainty "—I always want surprises."

That was news to him. He was a planner. Period. The idea of adjusting anything made his stomach ache or the claw climb his throat.

"I feel like there's a *but* there."

"Not really. The last time I was told there was a surprise, my parents were introducing me to the man they planned to marry me off to. Though technically, they told me there was a marriage contract, just not with whom. Maybe that means it wasn't really a surprise? In which case, this is my first surprise."

She blinked. "Rambly baby brain. S—" She smiled, catching the word before it exited her lips.

He shifted, pulling her just a hair closer. "That is one of my happiest memories." He'd nearly collapsed when his parents informed him what the meeting was. He'd only gone on a few dates with Kassie, but the idea of marrying anyone else was already impossible. The poet had captured his heart and soul. But he'd gone, unwilling, or maybe unable, to go against his parents.

An irony not lost on him since they'd tossed him out once she'd left.

Still, when she'd walked out with her parents, it felt like winning a universal lottery. Then he'd lost her.

"One of." She ran a hand down his cheek. "I know the top one. Getting the Nobel. I remember hearing your mother talk about it at dinner." She winked, then started to turn away.

"No." He lightly gripped her chin and waited for her to turn back to him. There was no way he was letting her believe that was his happiest moment. It might be his parents'; it wasn't his. "My happiest memory was you walking down the aisle." It wasn't a lie. He'd achieved so much. But the thing that made him happiest was her.

And I let her walk away.

Not again. He was winning her back and keeping her this time. Perfect partner, thy name is Apollo.

Never mind that he was sleeping less than ever. Staying up late to catch up on missed emails from meetings he'd shifted or canceled. Checking all the financial news, pushing reports out so they were in Henry's inbox when he arrived at work.

She was his. It was worth it.

"We're here." The driver's words echoed through the speaker.

She pursed her lips, her gaze not breaking his. "Where is here?"

"My home." He squeezed her as he felt her tense. "My new apartment."

"New?"

"Come on." He opened the door and pulled her with him to the private elevator. Entered his code and watched the doors close. He'd started looking for a place the second she'd mentioned that his old penthouse felt like a tomb.

He hadn't been able to get the description out of his head. The *very* accurate description.

"You bought a new penthouse or rented?" She stood next to him in the elevator, her head moving from the floor number going up and back to him. A look on her face he couldn't decipher.

"Bought. Plus, this one is more child friendly. There's a playground downstairs for when the weather is awful, and a park around the corner." He chuckled. There was no reason for him to rent. It was available with an excellent view. And no poor memories for Kassie. *Or me.*

"Bought." She whispered the word.

"Exactly. A fresh start." The door opened to his place. The place he hoped she'd come home to one day. "It doesn't normally look like this."

Kassie stepped inside, her face unreadable as she stared at the rows of clothes. "You mean you don't usually have racks of women's clothing strewn across the entire entry hall of your new place?"

There was a hint of something in her tone. Or maybe he was just reading into things. After all, she was overwhelmed.

"I made a call. Or rather a text." He'd told Emilio that he was sparing no expense. To tell the stores they had an hour to have it delivered. The private butler assigned to this penthouse had secured everything and disappeared the moment the driver alerted him that they were on their way up.

She looked at the racks. "This has to be three stores' worth of maternity clothes."

"Five. Technically. All rushed orders, which is why they are more than a little hodgepodge in here."

"Hodgepodge?" Kassie playfully rolled her eyes. "Not the description I would use. They are clothes racks for heaven's sake, Apollo."

He grinned. Given how this night had started, he loved seeing her playful. "I wanted the clothes here and everyone gone before we arrived. Our dinner will be here shortly but there are apples, cheese and nuts in the kitchen. Along with other things, but for a snack I figure those are go-to and easy."

"Orders?" She walked toward the first rack. "You ordered these? Like already paid for them?" There was that tone again.

Heat stole up his throat. But not the claw that had almost disappeared since she'd reentered his life. *Almost.*

Had he gone too far? Done too much? This was the easiest way to make sure she had everything—and more than—she needed right now. No more crying over unbuttonable pants. No more tight dresses, or panties that were digging into her sides.

She was sexy as hell. But when she'd pulled the offending pants down, he'd nearly cringed at how uncomfortable they looked.

"I mean, it seemed easiest." He pulled a hand across his neck. "Anything you don't like we will donate to a women's center."

"And what if I want it all?" She raised a brow. "Not that I can fit it in my place. My closet is a nice size, but not five stores' worth."

She didn't really want it all. He knew that. He heard the ask, or what he was hoping she was asking. "Then it can stay here. *You* can stay here. No pressure, Kass. This place has plenty of rooms."

"You bought a new penthouse, and five boutiques' worth of maternity clothes, for me?" There was a hint of something in her tone. Concern? Excitement? Fear? Amusement?

He wasn't sure.

"For us. Well, the clothes are yours. I don't think they'll fit me."

"For me." She let out a small sob.

"Kassie?" What if he'd overstepped?

She didn't say anything. She simply launched herself into his embrace. Wrapping her arms around his neck, she pecked kisses on his cheeks. "Thank you!"

Another kiss on each cheek, then one on his lips. Another, on his mouth, slower this time but still barely there.

He ran a hand along her back. Holding her still. He ached to deepen the kiss. Ached to close the tiny distance between their hips. But this was her moment. To do whatever she wanted.

"Apollo?"

His whispered name almost sent him to his knees.

"Kass?"

She swallowed, then pressed her mouth to his. This time there was no hesitation. Kassie drove this moment, and he was happy to simply be captured by it.

Her tongue traced his lips, begging for more, and he opened his mouth. The taste of her filling the empty place in his soul.

"Kassie." He ran a hand along the top of the sweatpants. The edge of the shirt just under his thumb. He slid a hand up, stealing the feeling of her bare skin.

The doorbell chimed and she jumped out of his arms. Pink flamed to red as she stared at him.

"It's dinner. And don't apologize. Please. That's the happiest I've been in forever." He reached for her hand, pulling it to his lips. He kissed each finger, then turned to answer the chime.

"Let them up, please."

"Apollo." Her soft voice was weighted with what he feared was uncertainty, or worse, regret.

"We need to get you fed, Kassie. Then you have to try on clothes, or pick what you want. Busy night." He grinned, hoping that his smile was realistic. They should talk about the kiss. But if she uttered the word *sorry*, it would break him.

CHAPTER SEVEN

I KISSED APOLLO!

I kissed Apollo.

The words were screaming in her head as she walked around the racks of maternity clothes.

Maternity clothes because I'm pregnant.

A new place...because I'm pregnant.

His lips were so soft. And because of that I'm pregnant!

Her mind kept ping-ponging between the kiss, the clothes and the new apartment. A new apartment. A child-friendly apartment. A place where he wanted her…but bought without showing her.

That happened in their marriage a lot, too. Apollo acted.

And I followed.

Just like growing up. Her parents issued an order and she got in line.

She'd broken through that over the past two years. Made her own life. Gave her own orders.

But how could she be mad? He'd seen a problem and solved it.

An apartment full of maternity clothes—in record time—for her.

And she *had* called their old place a tomb. So he'd found another…without telling her.

That was the sticking point.

Would I have come if he'd asked me?

Ugh. Her brain didn't have a rebuttal for that. Because Kass would have told him thanks but no, thanks.

Maybe. If he'd asked this week, she might have come.

Might.

So was she just looking for a fight?

Her father had accused her mother of that all the time when she was growing up. Her mother issued a grievance and he'd shoot back with the fact that she was just looking for a reason to pick a fight. And the truth was her father wasn't always wrong. Her mother used any excuse to complain that her life wasn't what she wanted.

But she wasn't willing to give up anything to chase the dreams she claimed to love so much.

Perhaps she was just looking for a reason to argue. Maybe she was just trying to punish herself for the impulsive kiss.

Which was silly when he'd held her so tight, let her drive the kisses. Let her be in complete control.

Though, if he'd deepened the kiss, she'd have ordered him to show her the bedroom. And he'd have come.

Her body was warm as she ran a hand over the

first rack of clothes. Mist formed in front of her eyes and she looked away. If she wasn't looking for a fight then this was the sweetest thing anyone had ever done for her.

"See anything you like? If not—"

"There is no *if not*. Please, if I can't find things I like here, I'm not trying." Her mother had loved to punish her father—not that her father had cared. Kassie's husband had done something sweet. Kind. She wasn't going to get angry over that.

"You quite literally bought everything in my size from every boutique carrying maternity clothes in the city." She playfully blew a kiss his way as she pulled a dress from the rack in front of her.

He tilted his head. "Then why the tears?"

She blinked. "No tears." Yes, her eyes were misty. A new apartment. A sweet gesture. The unfailing reminder that all this was happening because there were twins in her belly. It was enough to throw anyone off…even without the pregnancy hormones racking double time through her body.

But she'd let enough waterworks flow.

"I didn't buy from every boutique in the city." The muttered words were clearly meant to have a playful sound.

"Almost every boutique." She scrunched her nose as she looked at a dress. It was lovely.

"All right. Almost every one." He moved toward the rack. Toward her.

"What do you think of this?"

It was light blue, with ruffles and tiny hearts

that looked almost like polka dots if you weren't looking closely.

"I like it." He gestured to the dress. "Not sure I've ever seen you in ruffles, though."

She ran a finger under one of the ruffles. "My mother hated ruffles. So there was no ruffles in my closet growing up." *Or here when we were married.*

Those last words were unstated. Not because he'd done anything wrong. Apollo had never cared what she wore. Not because he wasn't paying attention but because he liked everything on her body.

The decision was hers. Though it wasn't until she moved out that she'd realized how much she was still trying to fit into the mold her parents had tried to craft for her.

She'd finally broken out of it.

And now I'm stepping right back in.

No. She was here on her own. By her choice.

Sure.

She pushed the tiny voice away. Kassie had no time for it. No desire to listen to its whispered worries.

"Go try it on." Apollo's words were light, but there was a tiny beat of heat behind them. Or maybe she just wanted there to be since her body still burned from the fleeting touches on her lower back. The taste of him on her tongue. "First room on the right down that hall is the master bedroom."

"You want a fashion show?" She said the words playfully as she grabbed a few other items. She expected a no. She'd made silly jokes like this throughout their marriage. And he always had something better to do.

"If you want to give one, absolutely."

Her mouth was dry. How many times had she joked like that and come up empty? So many. There was no annoyance, no flippancy, in his gaze. In fact, he looked genuinely interested.

She watched him swallow; a hint of nervousness hung on him. "Whatever you want, Kass."

Kass.

It had taken him no time to return to the soft nickname. The one she craved hearing from his lips. Maybe it was the hormones. Or the weeks of being at her beck and call, but for the first time in forever, the part of her that believed this might be able to work was larger than the warning signals her brain refused to fully mute.

"All right, but the second you are bored seeing the fashion show, you let me know."

"Not gonna get bored, Kass. Ever."

"We'll see." She wasn't sure if she was talking about the fashion show or their restarted relationship.

She stared at herself in the mirror. He'd actually watched the whole show. Clapped and cheered. It was silly and thrilling and she felt seen by…her husband.

He said he wanted her home. Wanted her here. Could they actually have a true second chance? Maybe. Maybe not.

Not that she was likely to come up with a decision while also questioning if she should actually walk out in the bathing suit she was wearing.

She'd grabbed the bikini by chance. She probably wouldn't get much use out of it. She wasn't allowed in hot springs with the babies and it wasn't like she had any trips to a sunny seaside planned.

Still, the fuchsia bikini was stunning. Kassie ran a hand over the bump where her children grew. Was it weird to feel sexy?

She'd cried because her body didn't feel like hers. It still didn't. But standing here, staring at herself in the mirror, the feeling faded to the background. She was growing two babies. And she felt attractive.

No. I feel hot.

Her chest heated at the idea of strutting out to Apollo. Watching his face and seeing if he thought the same thing.

"Everything all right?" As if summoned by her mental call, Apollo leaned against the doorjamb. "Damn." The last word was low. Guttural. And the heat in his eyes was liquid fire straight to her veins.

She bit her lip. "Just thinking the suit makes me look hot. Is that weird after I cried my eyes out over my body a few hours ago?"

"Not weird. And very accurate. *Very.*" He swallowed but didn't step away from the door. His gaze roamed her body, spending time on her breasts then moving lower. He was feet away, yet she felt like he was stroking her...with just his eyes.

Her body shouldn't heat from glances. Her heart shouldn't start to race or tell her to let go and see where this went. Her tongue shouldn't crave the taste of him.

"Shame I won't get to wear it anywhere." She sucked in a deep breath. It did nothing to quell the desire flaming to life inside her.

"Why not?" He slid away from the door, deliberate steps in her direction.

She ran a hand over the cups holding her breasts, enjoying the hitch in Apollo's breath. She was driving him crazy, by doing almost nothing. Their entire relationship she'd been in his thrall. The shift in dynamic was intoxicating.

"I'm not allowed in the hot springs. And hot tubs are out of the question. Even in the summer, the Baltic is cool." She shrugged. "Probably not a reason to keep the suit."

Apollo stepped in front of her. "My jet can get us many places where that suit will be perfect. So many options." His gaze dropped to her chest then floated to her lips and finally her eyes.

She lifted her chin. "You'd whisk me away on the jet. For a holiday?" They'd gone on their honeymoon. And a vacation for their five-year anniversary. But both of those were events that were planned months in advance to make sure that nothing interfered with his work. Even then, he'd had to do a few edits on a novel that was running a tad behind because of an editor getting ill.

Apollo *never* missed a deadline.

"Mmm-hmm." Apollo lifted his hand, but he didn't touch her.

"Did you even hear what I said?" Kassie ran a hand along his cheek, enjoying the power she had.

He grabbed her palm, planted a kiss in the center of it. "You asked for a holiday." Another kiss on her palm, then his lips brushed against her wrists. "Name the place. The time. I'm yours."

"Mine?" She raised a brow. Did he truly mean that? Any time? Any place…

His dark gaze met hers. His pupils dilated with desire. "Yours, Kass."

Tonight had come full circle. She was standing before him. In a bikini that revealed far more than his shirt and her panties had earlier. And need was nearly breaking her.

She didn't know what was happening between them. But tonight she wanted him.

Desperately.

"Apollo." His name was nearly a cry on her lips. "Kiss me."

He let out a soft moan. "Kiss you?" He pressed his lips to her wrist again. "Like this?"

A tiny shiver ran up her back. "No."

She felt him grin against her palm. He lifted his head, dropping light kisses up her arm, pausing at the sensitive spot in the crux of her elbow before moving to her shoulder. "Here?"

Her nipples hardened.

Apollo ran a thumb over each. Slowly. Barely there circles that drove the peaks higher. Pregnancy was already making her breasts tender, but the touch through her bikini wasn't nearly enough.

"You're toying with me." She started to reach for him—she was in control tonight.

His breath was already heavy. She loved driving him to the edge. Making him scream her name as he orgasmed. Tonight she was doing just that.

He sighed as her fingers brushed his length.

It was a dance their bodies knew. A script that played so well in the years they'd been married. And yet, something felt different.

Something was different.

Apollo's lips moved away from hers, and she let out a little huff.

"So impatient." He ran a finger along the tops of her breasts. The brush against her skin was a ghost. There but not. He was very good at driving her to the edge as well.

"I'm very patient." She reached for him again but this time he clasped her hand and spun her around.

"You're teasing me." She moved her hips against him. Two could play this game, and she was very aware how much he was ready for her.

His lips traced the back of her neck, along her shoulder, as his hand moved to her stomach. He palmed the bump then moved his hand back to her breasts. "Not teasing. Enjoying, Kass. You are here. You are carrying our children and you are mine."

Mine.

Her hips moved again, and she leaned her head back against his shoulder. "I think *you're* mine."

He spun her again; his hand gripped the base of her neck as he guided them to the bed.

"I am yours, Kass. Always."

* * *

Her lips against his. Her body beneath him. Her. Apollo grinned as the night's memories woke him. Kass.

He reached for her and found only a pillow.

A pillow?

An indentation was there, along with a long, dark hair. She'd been here.

She was still here. Probably just rummaging through more of the clothes he'd secured for her last night.

"Kassie!" He swung his legs over the edge of the bed, grabbed a pair of linen night pants and headed to the kitchen. She was pregnant, with twins; that meant the kitchen should have been his first thought. The babies seemed to crave food at all hours of the day.

"Kassie!" He tried to ignore the claw crawling up his throat. The penthouse was large. Not as large as his last one, but the view from this one was better. If she was here, she'd hear him.

"Kassie." Stepping into the kitchen he looked at the teacup sitting on the counter. Freshly washed. A plate drying next to it.

She was gone.

He took a deep breath. How many times had he slid from bed before she woke? How many times had she woken to no one?

The night of Arthur and Gemma's wedding.

He'd left. No note. No conversation. Just gone.

There was no shirt for him to pull the collar on.

Nothing to drive away the achy feel of anxiety as he looked around the empty penthouse.

Kassie was too kind to punish him. But the comeuppance was more than a difficult pill to swallow. He went back to the bedroom. Grabbed his phone.

Should he call? And say what? Why?

I never gave a reason.

Was this what it felt like for her? To wake alone? To experience the emptiness?

It feels like a tomb.

The claw tightened. She'd spent years feeling that way. Years alone while part of a pair.

Part of him expected to wake, pull her into his arms. Replay last night, then get breakfast.

No. All of him had expected that. Hell, he'd planned on scheduling movers. Bringing whatever she needed or wanted from her place.

And she'd snuck out without even a good-morning kiss.

He swallowed. He wanted her here. She belonged here. With him. He'd known it from the day they'd met at the writers' group. She was his. He'd let her slip away once. He wasn't going to—couldn't—let it happen again.

All right, the path to excellence wasn't completed in a week or two. He'd just need to work harder. Focus. Drive to the end. No mistakes.

What to do now?

He looked at the phone in his hand. Call or text?

Apollo had spent the entire evening worshipping

her body. It should not be hard to figure out such a simple action.

His thumb hovered over the call button before he switched to text.

Good morning, beautiful.

It was simple.

She responded back with a quick heart on the text.

He'd made contact. He'd get a few things done and then stop by during her lunch hour.

This was a marathon. Not a sprint, as much as he wanted it to be. This was a marathon. A marathon he was going to win.

"Is her lunch hour free?" Apollo smiled at Claire as he held out a pastry for her. A peace offering.

She looked at the pastry, then hit the call button on her headset. "Ma'am? Your husband is here with lunch. Do you want it?" He suspected her assistant wouldn't mind tossing him out, if Kassie ordered it.

She waited a second without breaking eye contact with him. "And do you want him with the lunch or should I take the offering and send him on his way?"

Apollo chuckled. "You're good."

Claire didn't respond to the compliment.

The door to Kassie's office opened. "Apollo? What are you doing here?"

The fact that it was still the tone of surprise...

Not a marathon.

"That dress is gorgeous." He grinned. "The blue ruffles are perfect."

Kassie laughed. "Luckily, there's tons of room to stretch. I think I'm bigger today than I was yesterday."

She looked at the to-go containers in his hands. "You really brought lunch?"

"I did." They'd eaten over his desk so many times. "Spend your lunch hour with me?"

"I can't." She held up a hand. "It sounds nice and I appreciate it. I do. But I'm not technically taking a lunch break. I need to go through a list of resorts in the Maldives. I have some clients who've decided to forgo having a big wedding here and need an exclusive location."

She looked at the to-go containers again. "That really does smell delicious. Sorry."

"Twenty-eight." Apollo winked. "Want help? I've been to the Maldives a few times." Always on business. Never the resort part. But still, he knew something about the islands. A little at least. He wanted to spend time with her, and if that meant sitting watching her work…or helping…he was here for it.

She rolled her eyes. "That sorry should not count." Her eyes danced to the food containers.

"We are going to differ on that. But seriously, do you want company? I can look at whatever ideas you have."

He heard the little whiff out of Claire's lips but ignored it.

Before she could answer, her stomach rumbled.

"All right. Bring the food. You can join me but when you're bored, don't blame me."

"Not going to get bored." He started toward her office and paused at the entrance. A huge screen on the wall was showing off a list of resorts with a color-coded system that had to mean something. "Whoa."

He wasn't sure what he'd expected but it wasn't this.

"Yeah. My system is a little messy, but it works." She clicked a few buttons on a device he hadn't noticed in her hand, and two more columns appeared.

"Don't do that." He closed the door and took the food to her desk to pull everything out.

"Do what?" Her eyes were glued to the wall, a tablet that had appeared from who knew where in her hands. She was taking notes and they appeared on the wall chart in one of the new columns. A set of codes that clearly aligned with cost, location and something else.

"Downplay your abilities." He took out the sandwich he'd ordered for her and the salad.

"Mmm." She took the salad, still looking at the wall as she ate the first few bites. Not a single comment on the self-deprecating statement.

How did she not realize how impressive this was?

"I can recognize the cost code and the location. What's third in that column?"

"Security." She tilted her head as she made another note and crossed a location off the list.

Security made sense. This was a high-end business. She had celebrity and aristocratic couples.

"So, this is a change? The wedding venue, I mean." He was not going to bring up the night they'd spent together. No matter how much he wanted to.

She squinted, like somehow looking at the board differently might make something clear. "Yeah."

Kassie made a few notes and then shook her head and struck two lines from her chart. "I only take on six clients a year. I am booked out for the next two years. And I usually have a venue secured eighteen months before launch."

"Booked out for two years? Wow. I mean, I thought our year-long engagement was long." Horrifyingly long. He'd wanted little to do with the wedding planning. Another thing he wished he could take back. All he'd wanted at the end of the day was her as his wife. He'd done damn little to make sure she knew that, though.

Kassie looked over her shoulder and offered him a smile. "A year is a baseline. These are high-end weddings with a starting base of three hundred thousand euros. I handle everything for them. Or my team does."

Apollo sucked in a breath. It was clear the place was upscale but part of him still hadn't realized how much she was doing as a senior planner. This was a different side of Kassie.

A side he wished she let out a bit more.

"I just finished my summer session. With six clients a year, I take on two each season. So this is my first fall, and then November, before my Christmas wedding. Then a break…"

The words dropped off. "Well, I've got Signa, my boss, taking on the clients I had scheduled before." She ran a hand over her belly. There was a subtle sadness in her smile.

She was pregnant. A thing he knew she'd always wanted, but that didn't mean everything about this was going to plan. Or that you couldn't have mixed emotions about change.

"So is this one in November or Christmas? 'Cause that's a big shift in just a few months."

"Neither. It's my fall one. Three weeks." The words were said with a professional tone that he had no idea how she managed.

"Three weeks! Kass." How was she not flustered? If Emilio heard such news he'd be panicking, and even Apollo's typical *everything is usually fine* would be rattled. Three weeks for a new wedding venue.

And she told him to fire unreasonable clients.

She shrugged. "I am hired to handle things. I handle them. I'll have two locations to pick from by the time lunch is over. I've already eliminated six countries and four resorts from the Maldives."

"Still, why not just go through with what they planned?" He hadn't paid a ton of attention to his wedding. *To their wedding.*

But surely, changing everything was too much to ask his wife.

"They're running away." She didn't look away from the list on the wall.

He looked to where her gaze was fixed. "Running away? To the Maldives?" Could you really call running to an upscale island resort *running*?

She nodded. "They'll have the civil ceremony here and then head to the Maldives for a very select group of people in attendance."

"Select? Meaning?"

"Not the groom's family." She let out a sigh.

Not the groom's family. He had issues with parents. Deep-seated issues. If he'd uninvited them to his wedding, they'd have never spoken to him again.

They don't speak to me now.

His throat tightened and he reached for his drink.

"Yeah. His family makes this a lot more difficult." The words were clipped but he wondered if there was a subtle dig on the other end. Kassie and his mother had never gotten along. Hell, his mother got along with basically no one.

"*Difficult* means they need to cut out a whole side?" Why was there a shiver running down his back? This wasn't his family. It wasn't his wedding.

"I make no statement on the guest list. What I meant was the groom's family has money and international influence. I ruled out the Seychelles because of family business connections. His parents would easily find them."

"Is there no way to work out the differences? I

mean, they are family." Seriously, he didn't know these people. Why was he arguing?

She tilted her head, but didn't look at him. "Family doesn't really mean much."

"What!" He pursed his lips. She was carrying their children. Their family. "How would you feel if our children did this?" Walking away was Arthur's choice. Choice. Apollo was thrown out. He knew how much that burned. How it made you feel worthless.

Her head snapped to him. "I would beg forgiveness for whatever I did to warrant such actions. I would tell them I love them and that I understand their choice and swear that I will work on myself to fix the issue. Then I would make those changes so my children *wanted* me in their lives."

She took a deep breath. "*That* is what I would do."

"Being cut off isn't fair." The words were out and he wished there were a way to pull them back.

They weren't discussing their families. Not really—except…

She set the tablet down and was at his side in an instant. "It isn't fair. You have every right to be angry but it is also exhilarating. If you let it be?"

"How can you say that?"

"Because you get to rule your life. With no unhelpful inputs. Your destiny is yours. Though, you and Arthur have already basically achieved *everything*."

"Not everything." He pursed his lips as the words flew out. He'd woken without her.

"Meaning?"

Apollo shrugged. "I didn't come here to fight." He'd left her so many mornings, he wasn't going to point out that he had everything but her. He didn't have everything until she was his…again.

"We aren't fighting." Her hand cupped his cheek. "A discussion is not a fight."

He pressed his lips to her forehead, his body relaxing as she melted into him. "Sorry."

"Three." She lifted her head and brushed her lips against his. "Careful. Your number is rising."

He chuckled, hoping it would force the claw away. It did…a little. He didn't want to discuss his parents. Didn't want to think about the fact that she was at least partly correct.

Without them, he could control his destiny. But the failure…the fact that they'd thrown him away. How could he be worth something if the people who'd made him who he was, forced him to succeed, no longer wanted him in their lives?

"Have you narrowed down your couple's new romantic location?" The shift in conversation was direct.

Her bright gaze captured him. He saw dozens of questions dancing there, but instead of traveling whatever that path was, she turned and looked at the list. "Not quite yet."

The conversation twisted to nothings. Fun stories and questions. But nothing compared to the sword he worried was hanging over them.

CHAPTER EIGHT

"HAVE YOU THOUGHT about painting this room?" Kassie walked over to the window of the penthouse looking out at the mountains. "The view is beautiful, and you just have white walls."

Apollo looked up from his phone. A few texts had arrived from the office. At least a dozen emails so far. A market shift in Asia was causing panic. Panic wasn't warranted. At least not yet, but people were emotional creatures.

Henry was handling it. Mostly. He'd fed into the panic a little but seemed to have calmed down. The man had done well, better than Apollo expected. But when nothing was wrong, it was easy. Times like these were when careers were made.

Henry was doing well enough…for now.

"Paint?" He looked at his wife, standing in the window; her loose brown hair was wavy in a cute, almost messy style. She'd been here every night.

And always left before sun was up. At least he'd walked her to the door the past two days, rather than waking to an empty bed.

"Yes, Apollo. Paint." She pointed to the wall and

then to the window. "See the snow tops on the mountain? They're the same color as your wall. And when winter comes, we will just be looking at a whole patch of white."

We.

She'd said it without thinking. He knew that.

His phone buzzed again and he swallowed the anxiety building. There was a limited time to calm clients. Once they were overexcited, they tended to demand financial changes that were bad for everyone.

But Kassie was here. And he'd sworn he'd be the best husband. Henry was handling it. He was handling it.

He was.

"Out with it." She crossed her arms.

"I haven't thought about paint. Is there a color you want?" He'd paint the whole place in the brightest, most obnoxious colors in the world if that was what she wanted.

She rolled her eyes and walked over to him. She bent over. The shirt she was wearing wasn't low-cut, but from this angle it did offer a nice look at her breasts.

His phone was out of his pocket before he fully registered her intent.

"I'm off the clock, Kass. I swear." He'd go back on when she fell asleep. It was the role he'd taken the past few weeks. Hold her until she fell asleep. Slip out, finish up work, then hold her close the rest of the night.

Her eyes raked through the phone. Other people might be worried about finding a secret dating app or texts from a lover. His phone was free of those betrayals. But the market notifications were lengthy.

"A bank failure in Japan." She nodded as she handed the phone back to him. "You should handle it."

He shook his head. "Minor bank." The phone buzzed again.

"Apollo, I will still be here. Go to the office and handle it."

He looked at her. "I am just going to the office down the hall." Here. He was here. But it would make life easier if he handled it now. "If you don't mind, just for a bit. My director is a little panicky."

She leaned over; her sweet scent would have driven him crazy if his mind wasn't constantly interrupted by the damn phone. "I meant the office here and I don't mind."

Kassie gripped his hands, pulling him from the couch. "Go. I want to go to bed at a reasonable hour."

"Define reasonable?" He held up a hand as her face fell. "Rhetorical question. Meant it to be funny. Maybe one day it will be."

"Maybe." She tilted her head. "But when we go on holiday, you are not taking that phone!"

"Deal."

"Coffee. Decaf. Because you do need to sleep

tonight." Kassie walked into the office and set it on the well-worn desk.

"Thank you, Kass. It won't be much longer." He and Henry had gotten nearly all the clients back on the same page. Only Roger was still hyperventilating. And he was to the point where there was little left he could offer the man.

Unfortunately, Henry was still intent on placating him. Which was actually drawing this out more.

"Heard that before." She walked over to the wall where his latest mystery book was plotted. He'd written a few thousand words in the past few weeks. Not enough to get back on schedule, but that was a problem for future Apollo. One he'd figure out.

"I mean it, Kass." He did. He was not going to spend more time on this than necessary. He'd spent so long tied to the desk. To his phone. To the whims of clients. Now he was making sure his wife was the priority.

The claw still threatened but it was easier to push it away now. Easier to focus on what he wanted. What he needed.

"I know." The words were light, but they meant the world.

He wanted to argue but Roger called and he answered. "Roger, you berated Henry for a solid thirty minutes. I will not have you speak to my employees that way. Nothing has changed. This is a hiccup."

He held out the cell as the man let out a tirade.

"You exhausted yourself yet?" Apollo pinched the bridge of his nose. He never handled clients like this. Ever.

But part of him just couldn't deal with Roger anymore. The man was making him pay attention to something other than the wife he was trying desperately to win back.

"This was a minor bank failure. It spooked the markets but they are already settling. There is no indication the issue will spread." During the 1990s, Japan had massive bank failures that crippled the economy and resulted in what the country called the lost generation.

They'd regulated and righted the path in the early 2000s. Apollo hadn't been alive for the bank failures that Roger was rehashing on the other end of the phone. There was risk in this business, and the bank failure was larger than he'd like. Ideally, Apollo liked to see no failures, but it wasn't cascading across the economy.

Roger was still going on and Apollo rolled his eyes. "Here is what is going to happen. I'm going to hang up. My wife is pregnant, tired and I want to join her in bed. I will get back in touch with you tomorrow at nine. Not a moment before. The last thing I'm doing before I head to bed, is alerting my team that they are not to take your calls for the rest of the night."

He was not surprised by the apocalyptic response, but he also had no interest in prolonging the discussion. "You are free to take your business elsewhere, of course." He heard a soft intake and turned the chair, catching Kassie covering her mouth.

"If you still feel that way at nine tomorrow, I will personally draw up the papers for the dissolution of our business relationship. Good night."

Kassie's eyes were wide. Her lips parted.

"I need to send three texts. I don't want my team listening to him any more than they have to tonight." He sent them then stood.

"Are you all right?" Her finger brushed his cheek.

"Yes." It was a weird feeling. He was waiting for the claw. For the worry. The pinch of anxiety that tended to pull him fully out of control. Nothing appeared.

"He'll bluster all night and by nine he will be willing to listen." Probably.

"And if he isn't?" There was worry caked in her gaze. Panic.

"Kass, he will be. And if he isn't, then I will do exactly what I just said and end the partnership. He's a big client, but the company will be fine without him." He said the words and once again waited for the fear of failure, the anxiety, the strive for perfection that had lived in his brain since before he could remember, to materialize.

All his mind could focus on was the woman standing before him.

Kassie smiled and turned toward the mystery boards. “You struggling with this one?”

“No.” He cleared his throat. “Yes.” What was the point in hiding it. “I can’t get the story right. Or rather, I can’t get my mind in the right place to figure it out. The words will come.”

Now the panic materialized. Writing didn’t pay the bills. Even hitting bestseller lists only made so much money. And nothing compared to the billions he’d made studying the markets, writing articles on the market, living in the market…basically.

Writing was his “fun” thing. His escape from the world.

“Writer’s block?”

“I don’t believe in writer’s block.” He’d heard others talk about it. But he’d never let himself give in to the idea. The words would come.

“You were worried about *my* writer’s block.” Kassie scoffed as she turned to face him.

Touché.

“Do you believe in burnout?” She laid a hand on his chest.

He didn’t want to discuss this. Didn’t want to broach the topic that was ringing in his ears. He wasn’t burned out. He was balancing everything just fine. He was.

“For others, yes.” He pulled her into his arms. “Do you really want to talk mystery plots, writer’s block and burnout?”

Before she answered, he ran a hand along her

cheek, a thumb along her lips. "Because I have many other ideas running through my head."

She looked over her shoulder, and he saw the hesitation before she looked back at him. "Do you?"

He bent down, picked her up in his arms, enjoying the tiny, excited sound escaping her lips.

"Apollo."

"I like it when you say my name." He used his feet to open the door to the bedroom. "I love it when you moan it."

"Don't go." Apollo's hands hovered on her hips.

Her skin still burned from his kisses. His attention. His heated words.

"Apollo."

He pulled on her hips, turning her to face him. Her breasts pressed against his chest. His breath drove goose bumps along her skin as he leaned toward her. "Stay."

She wanted to. Desperately.

That was the problem.

Once upon a time, all she'd wanted was for him to beg her to stay. Or rather for him to want to stay with her.

Now the words were there.

Even the actions. Over the past month, she could not fault him. He arrived when he said he would. He didn't have his phone in front of his face all the time. He paid attention. It was perfection.

So why was a not-so-small part of her still wanting to race out of here right now?

Because she still wasn't sure why he'd changed. No. That was the problem. She was. And it had nothing to do with her.

"You have early meetings and I have to finalize the details for Sven and Mara's wedding." The couple was heading to the Maldives this weekend. Everything was booked. Everything taken care of. One of the junior planners had traveled ahead this week to ensure stuff was fully taken care of. She was headed out on Thursday and back on Sunday after the Saturday festivities.

Part of her was tired just thinking of it. He'd said he was going with her. Using the private jet to get there. She was working all weekend but he was coming. Just to come, he'd said.

Stay.

Go.

Her heart and her mind warred with each other. In the end, her mind controlled her tongue. "I should get going."

"My first meeting isn't until eight. I'll get up with you if you want to leave early." His hand ran along her upper thigh.

"Apollo—" It was hard to concentrate when he touched her.

"Is this punishment?"

Ice splashed down her veins. She saw the exact moment he registered the question was the worst move he could make.

Didn't change the words or her immediate movement from the bed.

He was moving with her. "I didn't mean that."

"I think you did. I think that you think that you can spend a few weeks as the perfect husband and I will just run home and be the perfect little forgotten wife again. Acting the part I always play. And I can't even blame you for thinking it, because here I am. In your penthouse. A penthouse you bought for us without even asking me!" Her bottom lip was trembling as she pulled the pants over her hips.

She wasn't sure where he'd thrown her panties but she wasn't pausing to look right now.

"Kass."

She shuddered as the pet name fell from his lips. She stormed to the front of the penthouse.

"Kassandra."

There it was. A dividing line she'd thrown down. The one she'd lifted. The one he was putting back in place. It stung but she was not going to ask for the nickname back.

If he wanted to use it when they were fighting, fine. At least then it was easier to control the emotions that were spinning around her.

"What? What, Apollo? You want me to stay after you just asked if I was punishing you? You want me to ignore the pain of that question and just hang out? Sleep over and pretend that wasn't a knife to my heart?"

"I want you here. *Here.* Kassie. I moved. I left the penthouse. I got a new place. I am here. I am present."

Her heart squeezed. He was right. He'd done

those things. But not just for her. None of this was just for her.

"We're having children."

Her heart cried out at his words. The reason standing between them. The issue that her mind couldn't look past.

"Right. And that is why you want me here. You never would have reached out to me if I hadn't told you I was pregnant, would you?" She crossed her arms.

He just stood there.

"Answer me." He'd thrown the gauntlet; she was simply answering the challenge.

He opened his mouth, shut it, then opened it again. But no words came out.

"I swore when I woke up alone the morning after Arthur and Gemma's wedding that I wouldn't reach out. That for once I would let you reach out to me. That I would wait." She looked at the door then back at him. "So answer the damn question. Would I have waited forever?"

He swallowed. "I don't know."

She tilted her head and raised a brow. "Yes, you do. You just don't want to admit it to me."

"No." He shook his head. "No. You're wrong."

"You would have reached out first?" She wasn't sure why she was pushing this. Why now? Why not just walk out?

"No." Apollo closed his eyes. "No. I wouldn't have. But it's not you that I don't want to admit that to. Though, that is the case, too. It's me. Do you think I like the fact that I wouldn't have reached out? You think I like knowing I failed my wife? Failed my marriage? Failed at us?"

Failed.

The word rattled in her brain. Wiggling in the back of her mind, like an itch she couldn't scratch. But she wasn't sure why.

She bit her lip. "I think I should go." She'd started this. It needed to be said, but she didn't want to drag it out—as her father said to her mother. She'd made her point. Hurt them both. What else was there to say?

"No." Apollo stepped toward her but stopped a few feet away. "If you don't want to stay tonight, don't. But don't leave during the fight."

"Cooling off—"

"Is not what we do." Apollo closed the distance. "You know it. I know it. We say we are cooling off and then we just let it go. Pretend like it never happened."

That stung. But it was accurate. Their entire marriage she'd kept the peace. Refused to even partly act like her mother, who flew into a rage at the slightest provocation. That would not be here. But it also meant nothing was ever truly resolved.

"If that is what we need to do tonight, then let's do it. Fight and get it all out. You're still mad at me."

"No, I'm not." The words were very soft; even so, they tore through the room.

"Kassie."

“I’m not.” The truth burned as it left her lips. It would be easier if she was mad at him. Easier if she could wash away the pain with fury. But she’d never been angry.

Not really.

She’d accepted that she wasn’t what he needed. That she wasn’t a shiny prize so she got forgotten. It hurt. It tore her apart.

But she knew his parents. Knew the drive they’d instilled in him. Hell, her parents had tried very hard to make her the perfect daughter. She knew what it was like to walk away from family expectations. Build your own life.

Apollo had a wonderful life. A life created *for* his family. Not for him.

“Kassie.” He sucked in a breath. “Of course you’re mad. How could you not be?”

She shook her head. “That is the worst part. I’m not mad at you. Though your little quip tonight about punishing you was across the line.” She pushed away a tear.

“Then what is it?” Apollo put a hand on her waist.

He’d thrown on a pair of pants but no shirt. His hair was mussed from their lovemaking.

“What is it, Kassandra?”

“Why the full name?” She started to take a step away but he reached for her hand. “Anger makes it fall from your lips.”

He paled. That was unfair.

“I didn’t want you to think that I am trying to

win you over with the names only I use." His hand cupped her cheek. "Tell me. If you aren't mad, what is it?"

"I don't trust you." The words were daggers. She saw the moment they struck.

He didn't let go of her, though. "All right." He blew out a breath, but didn't step back.

Another tear slipped down her cheek. "I don't trust this to last. For you to be there. I don't trust that you're here for me. It's not really about me. It's for our children. Not me." The words were out. There was no taking them back. No recall. "Sorry."

"Twenty-nine."

Kassie didn't really think that one should count, but she wasn't in the mood to add that to the argument.

He ran a finger along her cheek, smearing the tearstain. "You don't trust this."

She sucked in a deep breath. "I keep waiting to wake up. Waiting to get left in the background again. For a bank failure, or market hiccup or deadline to suddenly take all the precedence."

While she'd never been truly angry when she'd stepped away, she'd been broken. Rebuilding was the hardest thing Kassie had ever had to do. She wasn't sure she would be able to do it again.

Risking it all was dangerous. Staying. Sleeping over was the first step. But if she took the first step, she'd take the next and the next. If it didn't work out this time, she wasn't sure how she'd rebuild.

Apollo nodded. "Okay. I won't ask again."

She bit her lip. “I’m not asking that. I want you to ask. I know I’m not staying. I know that. And I can’t promise when I will. If…”

Apollo pressed a kiss to her forehead, so light it was barely there. “Stay?”

“I can’t.”

“All right, then let me walk you to the car.” There was a sadness in his eyes, but he grabbed her hand and started toward the door.

“You don’t have a shirt on.”

“Perk of owning the building. I don’t think security is going to say anything.” He offered a wink.

The mood lifted. Just a little.

“Probably not.” They were at her car before she processed any time passing.

“Good night, Kass.” He brushed his lips against hers then opened her door.

“Good night.”

CHAPTER NINE

I DON'T TRUST YOU.

The words haunted his dreams. He heard them every time he woke in his empty bed. He'd honored his promise all week. He'd asked Kassie to stay. She'd told him no and he'd walked her to his car.

Part of him was frustrated. No, more than part of him. That was the problem.

Apollo rolled his head from side to side as he looked at the meeting schedule. He'd started working in the office two days a week.

He'd not missed it.

And he didn't know what to do with that.

This was where he'd lived for so long. The place he understood best.

The place that lost him Kass.

He'd worked so hard for his company. It should feel easy to step back in. To meet with clients he'd met with hundreds of times. Instead, he felt like he was walking in someone else's shoes.

"Ready for the next meeting?" Emilio straightened his tie as he looked at his tablet. The tie didn't need straightening, but that didn't stop the man from fiddling with it when he was nervous.

No.

"Yep." He started for the door. "You going to tell me why you're nervous?"

"I'm not."

"You are nervous." Apollo knew his assistant well. Very well. There was something the man wasn't telling him. "Out with it."

Emilio shook his head. "I want to tell. I do. But the answer is nothing. I just feel off. You ever had a feeling the day was going to go one way and then it just didn't?"

"No." Apollo didn't even know how to take the statement.

"I mean, come on, you are named for a Greek god that cursed a woman with premonitions." Emilio let out an uncomfortable chuckle. "You don't believe that you can just feel off?"

His parents had made sure both their boys had names "to live up to." He was named for the god of prophecy and light. Arthur for the mythical king. Neither of them was enough in their eyes.

Emilio let out an uncomfortable chuckle when Apollo didn't say anything. "Well, meeting time. With any luck, this day is nothing but a regular day."

Seriously, he did not miss the office. When he worked at home, he was able to take these calls and control when they ended. Here, the client felt like they were owed time.

"Is there anything else?" Apollo spun the pen in front of him. "We've gone over possible outcomes. I cannot make the investment decision for you. You have to make a choice."

How many meetings like this had he sat in? Hundreds? Thousands? This was his life. A life he'd worked hard for. A life he knew. And it felt empty.

A knock at the door, then a short blonde woman poked her head in. "Sorry, Mr. Nilson, there is a phone call for you."

"A phone call?" Roger Anders blustered. "He's in a meeting."

Apollo cleared his throat and shot the client a look. This was his office. He was in charge. "Who is the call from?"

"Your wife, sir." She took a deep breath. "She says sorry for bothering you but it's urgent."

"It will just have to wait." Roger pulled out a few more papers from his never-ending folder. Why the client thought he needed to bring every printout to this meeting was mindboggling. "We are not done."

"We are." Apollo stood. "I need to see to my wife." She never called the office. Never. That was a problem he should have rectified.

If she was calling now…

His stomach sank. The babies. Her pregnancy was progressing normally, or as normally as a twin pregnancy did. But they were inherently dangerous.

"You're busy." Roger shook his head. "She should know her place."

The words hit his heart. They were accurate. And heartbreaking.

She should. Kassie shouldn't be apologizing for calling his office. For any reason.

He looked at Emilio. "Please get Roger paperwork to cancel his accounts with us and transfer his holdings to the investment firm of his choosing by the end of the week."

Roger's hand slapped the table. "Hey, I am not canceling my account."

"You're right. I'm canceling it. We are clearly not a good fit." He'd done everything possible for the client. Everything. But he was not going to sit here and listen to more whining on problems that may or may not come to pass.

Emilio's eyes were wide but his fingers were flying across the tablet.

He stepped out of the office and took the phone from the young woman standing in the hall.

"Kass?"

"I probably shouldn't have bothered you. Not a big deal, really." She was rambling and her tone was off. Like she was groggy.

"She's in the hospital." The voice on the line was Claire now. Her assistant was at the hospital with her. Not him. "She didn't want to bother you, but she was feeling faint and they brought her to Karolinska."

"I'm on my way." He handed the phone back to the assistant. "Tell Emilio to cancel all my appointments for the rest of the week." He didn't stay back to make sure the message was passed.

He'd blown so many red lights on his way to Karolinska Hospital that he was certain traffic tickets would arrive but he didn't care.

He parked in the first spot possible and raced through the doors. "Maternity?"

The greeter offered him a smile and quick directions.

Apollo ran, not caring about the faces that turned to look at him. He needed to be with Kassie. Now!

He reached the maternity area nearly mindless. "My wife." He forced the words out between breaths. "Kassandra Nilson."

The nurse offered a small smile, one that he wasn't sure was meant to be reassuring or sympathetic.

"Is she all right?" The words were ash in his mouth. She had to be all right. The idea of the world without Kass…

Apollo couldn't walk through that reality.

"The doctor will talk you through everything." Rationally he knew that the nurse wasn't the one responsible for delivering diagnostic news. But Apollo had to mentally pull back the demand for more information. He was no good to Kassie if he was thrown from the premises

"Her room is this way."

The doctor will talk you through.

What the hell was that supposed to mean?

He stepped into the room and the world spun.

Claire was sitting on the tiny couch. Kassie was in bed, an IV in her arm. She was pale but awake.

"You got here quick." Claire looked at her watch. "Speed much?"

"Yes." He nodded to the assistant as she left the room. There was a hint of appreciation in her eyes. One that, if he wasn't standing in a hospital room with his wife admitted, he might have taken pride in.

Apollo moved to the bed, sat on the corner. "Kass?"

"It's nothing." She pushed a tear from her cheek. "I got busy with the wedding planning. A chef was fired at the resort yesterday. *The pastry chef.* I mean, I get that he was stealing money but he was supposed to make the wedding cake."

He took a deep breath to keep from cutting her off. She was working too hard. Trying to make sure she made partner.

Except part of him was worried that Signa had no plans to offer that. There wasn't a reason for the thought. Just an inkling he had from the few times he'd met her at the office.

None of that mattered right now. And he didn't care about the pastry chef. Hell, he'd personally fly one in. He needed to know about her. About their children.

Everything else didn't matter. Not right now.

"All right, you were focusing on fixing something." The fact that he kept his tone level, controlled, was a testament to the training his parents had imparted. No emotions. No celebrating wins or crying over failure. On to the next mountain.

"How did dealing with a fired pastry chef in the Maldives end with you here in the hospital with an IV?" He needed to know the problem. Then he would fix it.

She closed her eyes, tears spilling down them. "I didn't drink enough water. I have a water bottle marked with the hours. Twins suck up twice as much." She mimicked the voice of the OB they'd seen last week, who'd noticed subtle hints of dehydration in Kassie.

Nothing to worry over then, but she'd made a few recommendations.

"Okay. You weren't drinking enough fluid." That explained the IV.

Kassie hung her head, and he put a finger under her chin. "Hey, it happens." He wasn't sure how true that was, but she was upset enough right now.

"Not just enough fluid. Any." Her voice shook. "I got dizzy. Lightheaded. Like a brain fog that made words hard to reach. I know that sounds weird."

It sounded terrifying.

"Dehydrated." He said the word. He'd read so many books and online blogs regarding twin pregnancies. Dehydration was bad. Not the worst thing, but it could lead to that.

"All right, this is just a reminder, a scary one, that you have to drink enough, Kass." He reached for her hand. It was limp in his grip.

"I know. I know. I want the babies safe. But I just thought…" She pinched her eyes closed again.

"Thought what?"

"That I'd have more time." She opened her eyes; her gaze holding his. "The doctor is talking stepping back at work. She's talking about bed rest. I have a little more than six months to go. Five, probably, since the babies will most likely come early… and I had so many plans."

"If that is what the babies need…" He watched her shake as he said the words.

She ran the hand that had the IV over the expanding bump where their children were growing. "If it is what they need, I'll do it."

"But?" He heard the word hanging there unsaid.

"I just got my life. A life I built. One that is mine." Her eyes cut away from him and color slid up her cheeks. "I sound so damn selfish."

He squeezed her hand. She'd mentioned something like this when none of her clothes fit. He'd heard it, but he hadn't really understood.

"You just got your life." The words sliced his soul. *A life without me.* Those were words she hadn't attached but there was no way for his heart to unhear them.

"I built my clients. The firm was already there, but I made senior planner. I did that. And now…" Her thumb stroked her belly.

"And now you have to adjust."

She nodded. "I used to go all day without drinking. Hell, I had nights I'd get home from an event and realize that I hadn't had more than coffee for the day."

Apollo squeezed her still-limp hand. "That isn't ideal, either, Kass."

"Says the man who only ate dinner for a year because I showed up at the office and sat on his desk to make sure that he swallowed more than coffee for the day." She gave him a little grin.

"I'm stepping back some. There's nothing wrong with it."

"I was so close to making partner. Am so close. And you have a company. A whole company that you built. And you write bestselling mystery novels. Your life is exactly what you want it to be. I just started."

"Not exactly what I want it to be." He lifted her hand to his lips. But he understood. She'd had plans. And they were shifting.

"Do you want the babies?" He held up a hand. "There is no judgment in that question, Kass. This is not a small undertaking."

"I know." She pushed a tear off her cheek. "And the answer is yes. I knew the moment I saw the positive test. I always wanted to be a mother. It's a dream."

"But?" He squeezed her hand. There was no judgment but he wanted her to trust him enough to be honest.

"I just… I just still wanted to be me."

"Then you will be. I will make sure of it." He had more than enough resources to make sure she could do whatever she wanted. Rather than partner, he could make her CEO of her own event-planning company. What was the point of those resources if not to care for the woman he loved?

"You make it sound so easy." She rolled her eyes.

Whatever else she might say was cut off by the door of the room opening and the doctor stepping in.

Claire opened the door to her office, like she had every hour on the hour since Kassie arrived. "Have you drunk your water?"

"Yes."

Her assistant gave a little sigh. "Sorry."

"It's fine." Signa had tasked Claire and two other juniors with checking in on her.

She was also actively looking for someone to take the Maldives trip "off Kassandra's hands." Kassie had explained, more than once, that she didn't want it off her hands.

That was another worry she didn't have time for right now. The pastry chef had gotten canned and quickly arrested by the local authorities for stealing more than two hundred thousand euros from the resort over the past six months.

Six months.

How the man had expected that to go unnoticed was beyond her.

Unfortunately, there was a dearth of available pastry chefs, with the ability to craft a six-layer wedding cake, with less than forty-eight hours' notice.

Her bride was panicking. And Kassie was doing all she could to keep from falling into the same issue.

The door to her office opened. "I swear if you are here to ask if I have drunk my water, I will throw the now-empty bottle at you."

"Glad to know you are drinking." Apollo's words were soft; his deep tones settled a little of the anxiety clawing its way through her. "But I am actually here with a pastry chef."

"Pastry chef?" She turned, more than a little upset that a mythical chef wasn't standing next to him, cake in hand.

Apollo smiled, but the look sent chills down her spine.

What did he know of pastry chefs? Why was he even looking?

"I wasn't aware you knew anything about pastry chefs." She'd handled all social events. Many that he hadn't even made it to because a business crisis had taken precedence.

He let out a chuckle but there was a hint of worry in his gaze.

She took a deep breath. "Sorry."

"Thirty-two." He moved to the desk and leaned against it while she was standing in the center of the room. Lists of chefs on the wall, all with red crossed-out names. Hell, she'd even asked Anna.

Who'd gently told her that her skill level was not close to high enough.

And even if it was, her heart was in cookies and *kladdkakas*.

"I thought I was at twenty-eight." She crossed her arms. She should ask about the pastry chef, but part of her didn't want his help. This was her world. The place she'd carved for herself.

"You said it several times in the hospital." He pointed to the wall. "This is the reason I'm here, though."

"Not for me." She wished there were a way to pull the words back in as his dark eyes slid to her. It wasn't fair.

"Of course it's for you."

She bit back the sorry that was trying so hard to slip into the room. "You found a pastry chef?"

"I made a few calls."

A few calls. For a pastry chef?

"And you think you found one?"

He crossed his arms. "I did better than find one. I sent him to the resort this afternoon."

"Sent him?" She let out a breath. "You sent an unknown pastry chef to one of my weddings. Without telling me."

Color crept up his neck. "I figured since Pierre Oliver is world class—"

"Pierre Oliver?" She couldn't believe her ears. How was she supposed to get upset if he got the pastry chef everyone wanted and no one could have? "He's retired. And he told me no when my office reached out."

"Everyone has a price, Kass."

The words were tiny daggers. Not intentionally, but they were a reminder that he could have whatever he wanted. Could walk away and never work another day in his life and still have more money when he died than he did right now just because of interest accumulation.

Did he think she had a price?

She didn't want an answer to that.

"I can give you what we planned to pay him but I can't give you whatever obnoxious amount got him to agree."

Apollo waved his hand. "Not concerned with it." *Of course he wasn't.* "He's on his way. That's what matters."

"So you put him on your private jet?" It actually made her life so much easier. Part of her hated that. This was her problem. She should fix it. Instead, he'd swooped in.

"No. We need that. I put him in first class with a nice retainer so he could purchase anything he felt he needed for the trip. Figured the sooner he took off, the better." He grinned but there was something in his look.

An uncertainty. Apollo Nilson was never uncertain. At least he was questioning his decision. Maybe. Or maybe she just wanted to be asked before he pulled a trigger.

A trigger that might literally have saved the event.

Fine. She was going to roll with this. Because it did quite literally save the day.

"Well, that solves one problem."

Apollo raised a brow. "What's the other problem?"

"Signa is looking for someone else to take over the wedding." The words hurt to say. She put a hand on her belly, hoping touching the twins would help alleviate some of the pain that her career was facing, at least temporarily, derailment.

"Tell her you're going." He put his hands on either side of the desk. If the day hadn't been so stressful, and he hadn't sent a pastry chef on his way without even checking with her, she'd slip in between his legs and kiss him. The man was smoking hot.

A truth, even if the second trimester hormones were in full force.

"It's not necessarily that easy." Signa wasn't angry but she worried about the business. Their clients were some of the wealthiest in Europe. That also meant they were demanding and more than a little spoiled. They might be happy for her growing family, but deep down they didn't want it impacting on them.

She understood Signa's worries but she was more than capable of still handling everything.

"Are you or are you not a senior planner?"

"I am." She hated the pinch in her chest at the

question. He was right. She was a senior planner. There was no reason for her to step away from this event if she felt comfortable doing it.

He tilted his head. "So?"

He was right. She *was* a senior planner. This was her wedding. She walked to the desk, picked up the phone. "Signa, I am going to the Maldives. And the pastry chef is on his way now. Pierre Oliver."

She pulled the phone away from her ear as the shocked sound echoed out of the receiver. After waiting a second, she put it back to her ear. "Apparently, he isn't quite retired." Apollo really had saved the day. And the look of satisfaction he was wearing meant he knew it.

All right. It was a lovely gesture. Even if he should have checked with her.

"I will make sure that I take care of myself. Yes, I will drink plenty of water. I doubt that the junior associates will let me out of their sight."

"Neither will I," Apollo said.

She couldn't stop the smile that burst from her lips on that simple declaration. He was going with her. This was not something the babies needed. It was just for her.

For me.

She hung up the phone and looked at him. "Thank you. I truly don't know what I would have done without the help. There really is no one else."

He reached for her hand and pulled her to him. Right into the spot she wanted between his legs. "You'd have figured it out."

"Not so sure about that."

"I am." He pushed a loose piece of hair away from her cheek. "But technically, there is a finder's fee to pay for this."

She put her arms around his neck. "Really? And what do you have in mind, Apollo? I have a few more things to wrap up here before we get on the jet. I could make sure you feel appropriately thanked."

Kassie leaned toward him, but he pulled back. She did not bother hiding her displeasure.

"The doctor told you to take it easy."

"*She* told me to drink more water and take care of myself. Not the same." And it wasn't. She'd paid very close attention to the words the doctor had said.

Apollo ran a hand along her side.

Why was he stalling? This was supposed to be a playful flirt.

She stepped out of his hold and crossed her arms. "What do you want?"

And why is there a catch?

"A weekend. With just us. A full weekend."

"One weekend, Kass."

A sleepover. That was what he wanted. In exchange for a world-class pastry chef she could not have hoped to get on her own.

"It doesn't have to be soon. But a weekend for us at home."

"To get the nursery ready?" The question was

out. Maybe it wasn't fair but she needed an answer on it. Was this for her?

"If that is what you want. I was thinking dessert flown in from Paris. Fancy lingerie, a couple's massage in the living room. You deserve some pampering."

"Because of the babies?" Why was she still pushing this?

"Because—" Apollo took her hand "—of all the hard work you've put in. Because I spent far too many years not pampering you. Because I want to see you blissfully relaxed."

"Or as relaxed as these guys let me." She could see in Apollo's face how much he wanted this.

For me.

"Now, about that idea of finishing up a few things here quickly so we have a few minutes on our own before the jet takes off?"

He pulled her toward him, his lips capturing the tiny moan that left her mouth. "That sounds like an excellent plan."

CHAPTER TEN

KASSIE COVERED HER hand with her mouth and tried to make it seem like it was just a hand movement. She was exhausted. But everyone was already watching her like a hawk.

She appreciated the concern.

Mostly.

If she was honest, the attention was overwhelming. After a lifetime of wanting to be seen, to be first, it didn't feel like what she'd expected. Plus, there was an undertone of *don't worry if you can't do something* that she hated.

She'd started almost at the finish line in life's race. Kassie came from privilege. She understood that. Accepted it.

That didn't change the fact that her family saw her only as a pawn to advance their social status. She didn't get her own dreams. She abided by the family requirements or got thrown out.

But that was not something the world saw. What they saw was a woman who had it all handed to her. A woman who didn't have to work hard.

The illusion was one she feared she'd battle her whole life.

She'd earned her place in her company. Her position. Her career. She'd built that from the nothingness that captured her when she separated from Apollo.

Now he was back in her life. She was having their twins.

And life no longer looked like the plan she'd been forced to create for herself.

The yawn pulled at the back of her throat, and she turned her head farther to let that yawn out.

Apollo didn't look up from his phone, so she was pretty sure she'd gotten away with it.

"Everything all right?" Maybe focusing on whatever had his attention would force her exhaustion away. Or at least keep her brain occupied.

He'd been attached to the phone since they'd gotten into the back of the limo. Something she'd dealt with for years but felt oddly out of place right now.

"I'm trying to find a midwife to keep on staff." There were a lot of words he could have said, but those were almost the last ones she expected.

"For who?" She crossed her arms.

"You and the babies." He made the statement without looking up.

Obviously.

Once more he was acting…on her behalf. Shouldn't she at least be consulted in the idea? She lifted her foot and pressed it into his shin. Not quite hard enough to be a kick but not super-soft, either.

His gaze lifted. "Ouch."

She took the phone from his hand. "I don't remember asking for help finding a midwife to keep on staff."

Color slid up his neck. "You didn't. But you didn't ask for help finding a pastry chef, either. And look how well that worked out."

One save did not equal needing another.

"There is still the wedding to get through to determine how that goes. But—" she held up the phone "—I do not need a full-time nurse on staff. Where would they even stay?" The home she'd grown up in had a staff quarters. She saw her nanny, the cook and the gardener far more often than she'd seen her parents.

Apollo had a chef who came in early and left after making dinner. And a cleaning lady, again someone who came in, worked a few hours each week then left. If she moved into the penthouse, she had no plans to up the staff. She wanted her home to feel like a home. Wanted her children to *see* her.

Wanted to make sure they never felt like a burden. Like they were unwanted by their mother… or their father.

"I have suites on level ten. It's where Feya, the chef, is residing. Part of her compensation package. She says the commute is the best in Stockholm."

Kassie swallowed. He was planning for a life with her in it. She'd craved that for so long.

Without asking me.

The entirety of their marriage she'd wanted him

to think of her. He was. It felt bitter and spiteful to get angry at the actions now. But she should be included.

"We're here." The driver slowed as he pulled into the hangar with the jet.

Apollo got out of the limo, then held his hand out for her. She took it and wasn't surprised when he didn't let go when they were out of the car.

"I'll grab my bag, but please grab Kassie's. She's exhausted."

"I can carry my bag." She started to reach for it, but the driver already had it.

Apollo grabbed his wheeled carry-on. "Of course you can. But why, when I can make sure you don't have to? And I noticed that you didn't argue that you weren't tired."

Part of her wanted to make a face. The juvenile gesture might feel good in the moment, but it wasn't going to do anything. "I had a long day. And we still have a fifteen-hour trip in front of us. Of course I'm tired."

She let out a sigh. "And yes, part of it is that I'm pregnant." She slid into the seat. "I'll take a nap before dinner. Happy?" As soon as they were in the air, she'd head to the private sleeping quarters.

"Of course." He dropped a kiss on her cheek then slid into his own seat. "But it has nothing to do with you admitting you're tired."

He reached for her hand. "I want you to know there is a doctor on the flight. We have our own spaces and I hope we don't see him. But technically, he is here."

"For the babies." She ran a hand over her belly. She understood it. She really did. It was sweet. The right move, given that she was pregnant with twins and headed on a long flight. She was in her second trimester. Still perfectly fine to fly, but the precaution was a good one.

As was the midwife.

All precautions her husband was paying attention to. All things that he'd planned. Without her asking. All things that she wouldn't need if she wasn't pregnant.

I wouldn't be here if I wasn't.

She bit the inside of her cheek. She wanted to be here. And Apollo wanted her here. That counted for a lot.

But did it count for enough?

"Kass." Apollo's voice crested over her as she reached for him. The figment of the man disappeared as she touched him and she felt herself frown.

"Apollo?" She reached again, but once more he faded out of her fingers. It was like her mind could conjure him but couldn't keep him. Her heart screamed as he reappeared farther away.

Why was he so far when she wanted him close? Heat warmed her cheek.

"Come on, Kass."

This time when she reached for him, her hand

wrapped around his. She opened her eyes and smiled. "You kept disappearing in my dreams."

He ran a hand along her arm and she sat up, stretching.

"Tell me that—" she pointed to the tray behind him on the desk "—has my dinner in it." Her stomach rumbled as she sat all the way up and stretched.

"Nope. It has *our* dinner in it."

She blinked a few times, then looked at her watch. "You must be starving."

He pulled the silver domes off the trays and passed her one. "Dinner in bed?"

"Seriously—" she took the tray from him as she crossed her legs "—did you really not eat?"

Apollo took the first bite of his steak, the look of satisfaction on his face confirming that he had waited.

"Thank you." She took a bite of her steak, and the dinner was gone before she realized. Then the yawn set in again. "Honestly, I know all the books and blogs and podcasts say I will be tired, but I could literally fall back asleep right now."

"You can go back to bed." He pushed the cart of food out the door and was back in a second. "We still have hours to go."

"I think I'll watch a movie." She pulled the remote off the counter beside the bed and scooted over. "Join me?" Kassie held her breath for a second. She'd popped so much popcorn in their old place, asked him to stay and watch a movie. He'd always been too busy.

She could see the memories floating through his mind, too.

Or maybe he was just trying to decide if what she wanted to watch was what he wanted.

"No disaster movies." Apollo started to slide into the chair across from the queen bed.

She scooted over, patting the place next to her. "No disaster flicks, huh?"

He slid in next to her, put his arm around her shoulder and let out a soft sigh as she laid her head against him. It was a sweet pose. Nothing sexual. But somehow, it felt more intimate than what they normally did in a bed.

"I hate them. The people in them always make the wrong choices."

She let out a giggle as she looked over the film choices. "If they made the right moves, the movie would end at the first act."

"I know. But seriously!" He squeezed her shoulder. "The same reason you hate rom-coms."

"I don't hate rom-coms." She playfully punched his stomach. "I just think most of them rely too much on something that could easily be fixed with a conversation."

He shrugged. "It seems that way but conversations are hard. As humans, we avoid them because we don't want to risk what we have. Or we're worried that the person we're talking to won't hear us. A conversation can fix everything, or cement that everything is irreparably broken."

She swallowed. He was right. And she wasn't

100 percent sure he was only talking about rom-coms.

"Very serious, Mr. Nilson. But I could say the same about your disaster flicks. They make dumb moves but when humans panic, they aren't able to think clearly. They react instead of thinking. Same theory."

"True." He kissed the top of her head. "So no rom-coms and no disaster flicks. What does that leave us?"

"A drama that is certain to make me cry, hormones or no. Or a comedy."

"Comedy," they said at the same time.

He wasn't sure what he'd expected to see Kassie doing as the wedding planner, but it was stunning to watch her command the whole room. The earpiece she gave commands into, the tablet she kept in her fingers at all times.

This wasn't her wedding, but she commanded every movement.

The pastry chef's cake was a work of art, but the florist had forgotten flower petals for the flower girl. Kassie had meticulously pulled petals from flowers around the venue. One or two here, another three there. Enough to fill the basket, but no flower looked like it had taken a sacrifice for it.

Then one of the servers failed to show. She'd instructed the team on how to shift so no part of the reception room felt empty from the floating trays of appetizers.

She was visibly pregnant, in a floor-length green dress that accentuated the bump. She blended with the guests, allowing her to flow through the room without being an obvious worker.

Invisible, unless she was necessary.

It was a skill. One he feared her parents had helped her develop and their marriage had honed. She was an expert at sliding away. At taking the backseat.

He'd underestimated his wife. Not intentionally, but it had happened anyway. But he wondered if she was underestimating herself. Did she really want to work for someone like Signa? Someone who dangled a promotion but wouldn't commit? If she worked for herself, she could control everything. And she'd be perfect at it.

This was a side of his wife he'd never seen. She was in command. In control. Everyone answered to her.

The woman transformed when she was in this role. No apologizing. She just took control.

The party was winding down. The DJ was playing the last song. He wasn't an expert but it seemed like this was a success.

She took a deep breath as he stepped next to her.

"Nice work."

"Thanks. As soon as the couple walks out of here, my portion is basically done. The junior employees will make sure everything is cleaned up. The good thing with Signa insisting on them being here is I don't need to be an extra set of hands for that. I just have to do the walk-through at the end to make sure." She tapped her hip against his. "The pastry chef saved the day."

"Oh, I think you had this more than under control." There she was again, downplaying her hard work.

"Any chance I can convince you to stroll with me on the beach while this wraps before you do the final shutdown? There's a small inlet just down the way." He'd found it on a stroll while she was getting everything set up.

He saw her look around the room. "We will be less than a five-minute walk from here." If she couldn't go he wouldn't push, but she'd just said her extra set of hands wasn't necessary.

"Okay. I'll meet you outside in a few minutes. I need to get the bride and groom off." She gave him a brilliant smile then headed out.

He ducked out and walked to the beach. The moon was full. The couple might have had to adjust everything at the last moment, but they could not have asked for a more beautiful place to get married.

Kassie strolled up to him, her heels in her hand. "Sand is not made for these." She winked and tilted her head. "Where is this inlet?"

Apollo held out his hand and felt whole as she laid her hand in it. "Follow me."

"Always."

The single word hit his soul. It was what he wanted to hear and also somehow not. He'd been the leader in their marriage. The one with the career that ruled everything. She'd supported him in everything. It was past time he did the same for her.

"You were amazing tonight." The ease with which she'd handled the evening looked effortless, but he was very aware that wasn't the case.

"Just doing my job."

He pulled her into the moonlit inlet, enjoying the hitch in her.

"Oh my." The water lapped into the tiny tide pools, and in the evening shadows, creatures invisible in the daylight shone.

"I can't believe no one else is here." She dipped her foot into the edge of the ocean and sighed. "The water feels amazing."

"I might have reserved it for the two days we are here." He pulled her close, catching the soft scent of perfume in her hair.

"Reserved it?" She looked up at him.

"Uh-huh. I figured it could be your little private retreat." The price tag was steep but Kass deserved a place to relax. Even if she only made it out here tonight. It was here. If she needed it.

"Retreat?" She kicked her feet, splashing water up.

"Yeah. There is a mini fridge stocked with your favorites over there." He pointed at the rock bank and well-camouflaged snack bar. Technically, you could request a bartender out here, but Kass couldn't drink.

"My favorites?" She raised an eyebrow and started toward the snacks.

He'd spent the past three months making sure he knew everything she liked. He'd talked to the chef, charted what was in the fridge and what disappeared fastest. It was a shame he hadn't paid attention sooner but he was now.

She opened the fridge and let out a little squeal. "These are my favorite!" She spun. "Thank you. This is perfect."

"Perfect?" He took a grape out of the ornate bowl the resort placed them in. "My favorite word."

Her smile faltered for just a moment. "Perfect is important to you, isn't it?"

"Some might say it's what I was made for." He winked.

"No." She put her grapes down. "No one is perfect, Apollo."

"As close to it as possible, then. Perfect husband. It has a nice ring to it."

"Apollo—"

There was a hint of something in her tone, something he didn't want to listen to when everything was going so smoothly. "What is the weirdest thing you've ever seen in this industry?"

"What?"

He popped another grape into his mouth then passed her one, savoring the feel of her lips as they brushed his fingers. "You know, like wedding crashers. You ever watch someone stand up when the preacher asks if anyone has any objections?"

That was huge in the movies.

"That tradition is largely obsolete now, but yes. I have had more than one crasher."

"Really. A last-ditch romantic gesture?"

"It's not romantic." Her tone caught him off guard. "It's cowardly. You make the ceremony about you. About your wants and needs. *If* someone has something they *need* to say, then it needs to happen before the ceremony."

"What about a parent who is worried?" He was stunned she was so rigid in this.

"That's worse." She let out a heavy sigh. "I've seen this enough in the industry but also in society. Do you remember Elsa Borg? She had a full scholarship to study painting in London. As if she even needed the money. Her parents married her off to an old aristocrat to ensure who knows what. Hell, our own marriage was arranged to satisfy our parents. The fact that it worked out and we fell in love is a miracle."

The world stopped on her last words. "It worked out?"

She grabbed a *kladdkaka* and popped it into her mouth. "I can't believe these are here." She looked at him and smiled.

What was the point of chartering a pastry chef to the Maldives if he couldn't also put his wife's favorite treat in her reset place?

He reached for her, pulling her to him. "I'm glad you like the pastry Pierre made, *amore*." He pushed back a piece of hair that had slipped from the fancy updo. "But we are not glossing over the *it worked out* statement."

"*Amore?*" She raised a brow. "You've never called me that."

He pulled a little closer, enjoying the feel of her baby bump, the brush of her breasts against him. "Then that is a black mark on me." Dipping his head, he kissed her.

He wanted to whisk her up to her hotel room. Strip this dress from her body and worship her all evening. But she needed to close up the wedding still.

Later, though.

As if this universe heard his thought, her hip buzzed. "I guess I'm needed back. Thank you for this. It was perfect. I can't wait to see it. In daylight."

She grabbed another pastry, popped it into her mouth and made such a satisfied sound it sent heat from the tip of his head through his toes.

This was perfect and he would be, too.

CHAPTER ELEVEN

KASSIE LOOKED AT the closed venue and smiled. She usually ended these exhausted and starving. Apollo setting up that little retreat meant she was *only* exhausted and hungry. Because these days she was always hungry.

Part of her had wanted to delegate the final walk-through to a junior employee. She could have. Signa always did. But she had to complete the job. To perfection. No one could doubt that she was good at what she did.

Pregnant or not.

Tonight should prove that. Her couple was happily tucked away in the honeymoon suite after redesigning the entire thing in three weeks!

She'd celebrate that coup tomorrow. Right now a shower, a snack and her pillow. In that order.

And Apollo.

After stepping into the elevator she pulled off her heels and tried to ignore the pain in her pinky toes. Her feet were a tiny bit swollen. Standing in the ocean had helped, but the relief had been short-lived when she washed her feet and put the heels back on to finish everything out.

It wasn't surprising after running the event for the past ten hours but it was another thing to keep an eye on.

Another reminder that she was going to have to adjust.

Weird how her entire life she'd wanted to be a parent. She'd brought it up with Apollo a few times, but something had always come up before they'd had a full discussion.

She'd been so frustrated with him. But part of her understood now—a little. Kassie wanted to be a parent but her career had a place, too.

Balance. It all came down to balance. Which Apollo was much better at now.

Apollo.

She'd told him their arranged marriage had worked out. That they'd fallen in love. A truth, and one she wasn't sure she was ready to discuss yet. Which was why she'd bolted back to finish up the final wedding details.

She got to the hotel room, already thinking of what snack she'd order from room service. She should have asked Apollo to bring her something from the inlet he'd rented.

For her. A retreat for her. It was so sweet.

And probably what she'd dream about tonight.

Opening the door, she blinked; the room service tray was already in the suite.

"Apollo?" Kassie waited a second, sadness gripping her as he didn't pop out and yell *surprise!*

You got me room service but didn't stay?

She added a little sad emoji and hit Send. She practically danced over to the food. Fruit, cold sandwiches and cold steak, already cut up to go on the salad. It was more than she needed after the treats on the beach.

Her stomach rumbled. *Or maybe not.*

"When you guys are born, we are going to have a little chat about the meat craving."

A knock echoed through the room and she walked over while eating the salad. She opened the door and smiled at Apollo before taking another big bite.

She beamed and beckoned for him to come in. "Thank you for having the food here. I shouldn't be so hungry."

He shrugged.

She waited a minute for him to say something about needing to snack throughout the event. To shift the focus from her to the babies. He wouldn't be wrong. But everything just moved so fast.

Instead, he ran a hand along her cheek, before touching the earpiece she'd forgotten was still there. One got used to it when it was in all the time. "I will admit to being more than a little turned on when you have that earpiece in."

She laughed as she walked back to the food. "An

earpiece. Who knew that would turn Apollo Nilson on?"

He slid into the chair next to the room's small desk. "It's not the earpiece. Or not just the earpiece. You are confident when it's in your ear. Like you know exactly what you're supposed to do. I suspect you didn't apologize once today."

"Not apologizing is not a flex." She took a bite of the sandwich.

"You know exactly what I mean." He raised a brow. He'd changed into linen pants and soft T-shirt that hugged him in all the right spots. The tux he'd had on on the beach was magnificent. But this was perfection in a different way.

She knew exactly what he meant. When she was at an event, she was in control. People looked to her for guidance. She was the final stop for questions. The one with the answers.

It was the only place like that she had. It was intoxicating.

"I appreciate the food, at the inlet, and here. And now—" she turned "—any chance you'd unzip my dress so I can shower?"

Apollo was on his feet in an instant. "Of course." He leaned close as his fingers unzipped the dress. "You were magnificent tonight."

"I know." She leaned her head against him. "It was a lovely evening, but now that there is enough food in my belly to quiet the twins, I can feel the crash coming. Hell, even washing my hair is so much. You don't realize how tiring it is to carry flowers everywhere."

She giggled. "Wedding planner problems. Maybe you should shower with me and wash my hair."

"I'll get the water started." He pressed a kiss to her neck then walked into the bathroom.

She stepped out of her dress and walked to the bathroom. "It's fine, Apollo. Really, I was kidding." *Mostly.* Every muscle in her body was exhausted.

He started the shower and turned to her. "Kass."

She nearly crumpled at the soft look in his face.

"Say the word and I go. But let me take care of you." He put his hand under the water. "It's warm. Do I go?"

She shook her head; he stripped and stepped into the shower behind her.

She wet her hair, her arms achy as she raised them above her head.

"Turn around." The words were soft as the water hit her face.

She turned and felt his fingers run through her hair. Suds built as she leaned against him. "That feels so good."

"Good." His fingers didn't stop massaging her scalp. "Turn."

She did and started to lift her arms again. He gripped her hands. "Let me."

Slowly, he took care of her. Washing her, holding her in the warm water as her achy muscles relaxed. When he shut the water off, she let out a tiny groan.

"You need sleep."

He wasn't wrong.

She dropped a T-shirt over her head and slid into bed. Tomorrow her hair would be a mess, but she'd deal with it then.

"Good night, *amore*." The whispered words were already distant, her mind barely able to keep her eyes open.

"Apollo?"

"Yes?"

"Stay." The word was out, and as he slid in next to her, she laid her head against his shoulder and gave in to the exhaustion.

Stay.

Was there a more beautiful word in any language? He didn't think so.

He'd convinced her to stay with him in the Maldives. They'd had a couple's massage, a very careful one for her given the pregnancy, and frolicked in the ocean. Eaten as much food as possible. He'd even paid Pierre to stay on so Kassie could have whatever dessert she craved.

Today was their last day.

He wasn't ready to head back to Stockholm.

This felt like a dream. Every night he asked if she wanted him to leave, and she'd never sent him away. She'd curled into him, woken with him.

Stayed…with him.

Your father and I would like you to come to dinner. Both of you.

He blinked and barely resisted pinching himself

to see if this was a dream. They hadn't texted, or spoken to him in over two years.

He and Kass were in a good spot.

A great spot.

He didn't want to deal with his parents. It was a weird feeling. He was who he was because of them. He'd been hurt—was hurt—because of their reaction to Kassie's leaving him. Now she was back, and they were, too.

Just don't respond.

They made me.

That was the argument that his brain always countered with. Everything he was he owed to them. Sure, their methods had sucked. And they weren't going to win any parenting awards, but he and his brother were billionaires. Apollo had a Nobel in Economic Sciences, was a bestselling mystery author and his marriage was finally right where it should be.

If they hadn't pushed…hadn't demanded, what would he be?

He was behind on things right now. Sliding further behind the longer they stayed here, but he couldn't—wouldn't—rush Kassie.

"Apollo?" Kassie stepped into the suite, her tiny bikini already on. "You sure you don't mind missing the pool?" The hotel had a heated pool. One they claimed was less than thirty-eight degrees Celsius. But it sure felt warmer. They'd spent most of their days lying in sand in the inlet he'd made sure no one else had access to.

"Yeah, I don't mind missing the pool at all." He wasn't risking her or the babies' health. Plus, he liked having her to himself.

"Something's wrong. Did the office call? Is it some office emergency where people with too much money complain about not having enough money?"

Apollo nearly blew out the drink he'd just taken. He swallowed then started the chuckle. "No." Though she wasn't that far off with his clients.

"Is it the mystery you're behind on?"

"I'm not—" He stopped as she raised a brow.

"I saw your schedule. You are, which means I know you need to work all week on it to make deadline. So you should get to go where you want today."

She was trying to slide back. He'd caught this a few times. When she was in wedding planning mode, she was in charge. In control. In their marriage she accepted taking a backseat.

"We are going to the inlet. And—" he swallowed "—it wasn't the office." He was still working most nights when she was softly snoring. Catching up on nearly everything.

"Your mother." She said the words with no inflection. A simple statement.

"She texted." There were more words to say. Better words.

"Did you respond?"

"Not yet." He saw a look pass over her face. "I guess she heard we're back together."

"And is intruding. That feels so much like our wedding. And honeymoon, actually."

"She didn't intrude on the wedding." She had interrupted the honeymoon. Several times. Urgent messages about literally nothing. She'd wanted access to certain financial accounts. Wanted them to commit to attending a ball. Nonsense, but reminders that he was expected to answer to her even though he was now married.

He'd finally had to tell the front desk that he'd pay them not to deliver another.

She reached over to clasp his hand. "Your mother threw a fit because my father didn't attend."

He didn't remember that.

She leaned back in her chair, stretching her hands over her head. "Our cake was the wrong flavor."

"The cake was delicious." That he remembered. "Vanilla and strawberry."

She nodded. "Yeah. But the middle layer was supposed to be chocolate with a mint filling."

"I didn't know that." He'd missed the cake testing. A meeting had come up that at the time he felt he couldn't miss. A moment forever lost with her.

She shrugged, like all of this was no big deal. "Your mother contacted the baker. Not sure how she managed to get it switched."

"What?"

Why was he just hearing about this?

"Yeah. She was very proud of it. Told me that mint chocolate was trashy." She said the words with no animosity. No heat. Just a recitation of facts.

"Trashy!"

"Her words." She held up a hand. "Are you answering her?"

No. They were not sliding past that statement. "Why am I just now learning any of this?"

She tilted her head, a look of genuine confusion on her face. "It didn't matter."

"Like hell it didn't. You had the wrong cake because my mother threw a fit." The worst part was she hadn't told him.

He hadn't been the perfect husband. Far from it, but she'd never told him. Never explained what had happened and given him a chance to rectify it.

She walked to him. Or more of a waddle with twins pressing against her. She ran her hands through his hair. The touch so light.

"It didn't matter." She laid a finger over her lips. "All I wanted was to be your wife. The ceremony was a means to that end, but I loved—love—you. I didn't care about the cake. I didn't care that she was mad my father chose a business meeting over the wedding."

Loved. Love.

She'd started with past tense. Then slipped into present and then said something about the cake. Slid right past it.

Words were caught in the back of his throat. He wanted to scream that he loved her. That he was lost when she wasn't by his side. But he also didn't want to highlight something if she'd slipped into present tense only to not hurt him.

"I don't deserve you." He held her tight. There were so many words he wanted to say. But he stuffed them down. Until he was sure she meant it.

"You don't." The words were playful. Her hands ran through his hair, before she lifted his face. "But you are the one I want."

He still didn't deserve her, but he would. He'd make sure of it.

CHAPTER TWELVE

Henry made a mistake.

I think we need to look at the Miller account.

He overestimated the rate of return.

Leaving him in charge was a bad move.

THE TEXTS AND emails started as soon as their private plane touched down yesterday. Henry wasn't in charge. He was simply taking meetings for him. Though the fact that more than one person indicated they felt he was in charge meant that Apollo had lost the narrative that Henry was simply taking meetings when he wasn't in the office.

Which was a lot recently.

Not a lot. He was always available. Unless he was with Kassie.

So he wasn't as available.

This was a balancing act. He knew that. He'd focused too much on his business ventures before and lost her. She was home. In his arms every night. Pregnant with their twins.

He loved her. And if she told him she loved him, in the present tense, he'd shout it to the world.

Apollo felt like the entire universe was pulling him in every direction. He could not lose sight of everything. He would be perfect.

Perfect CEO. Perfect Husband. Perfect Father.

He just needed to rebalance everything now. Keep it stable.

This was the moment where he shone. Creating a company, running that company, writing, being the best husband and father. Everything was a priority but that was good.

He thrived on stress. It was how he'd grown up. In a house where stress was as much a friend as any buddy he met in school. Apollo was more than capable of handling everything.

The claw crept up his throat. *Breathe.* The mental order did nothing to stop the chokehold's grip. Running through his to-do list wouldn't calm him, either. Usually, it was easy to see what things were quick kills. Or basically already done. But right now his to-do list was seemingly ever-growing.

He wouldn't trade the days in the Maldives that had seemed to shift everything. Kassie was there. Every night. In his arms.

But it had set his schedule behind.

One step. He needed to just take one step and then another. The claw didn't recede, but he'd worked through its attacks before.

He sent off a quick note, and a response popped back immediately. A response that added at least three more items to his to-do list. Apollo let out a frustrated sound. He'd been at the office all day. In meetings all day. And somehow, the problems seemed to have multiplied.

And on top of everything else, this panic meant he was even further behind on his book. He was going to have to work straight through the weekend and forgo most sleep for the next few weeks if he was to deliver it on time.

Every deadline had crept a little further up on him over the past few years. But he still always got it delivered at least a week or two ahead of time. His agent was already pestering.

And cautiously asking if there was a problem with the manuscript…or with him.

Burnout was a thing every writer feared. But he wasn't burned out. Just a little overcommitted.

I could still ask for a push.

But his agent had already reached out about title queries. Hard to title a book when there were still a few thousand words left to write. *Or twenty thousandish.*

Rather than sending off a quick here-are-some basics, Apollo had pushed off the answer. So long that a follow-up email arrived this morning.

It's not like you not to respond.

The opening words had sent his head spiraling.

Every second of his day was packed. And there were only so many hours to work through the stack.

So many stacks. He just had to rearrange the bits. Find a way to get everything in order. He was more than capable of being the best at everything. He *was.*

I have to be. Failure isn't an option.

Failure lost you everything. It cost his brother feeling loved as a child. It cost Apollo his wife… and his parents. He couldn't lose her again.

"If you frown any harder at that phone, it might break just to avoid the upset look." Kassie walked over and reached for his phone.

He immediately pulled it back.

Now it was his wife frowning.

Most women would assume that meant a cheating spouse. There were viral social media videos of women walking through that nightmare. Luckily, he knew Kass wouldn't suspect that.

Didn't change the disappointment rolling through her features or the fact that he knew why she wanted the phone.

"Give me the phone, Apollo. You need to eat." She held out her hand. "It's ten. Well past dinnertime. I know you didn't eat at the office."

It wasn't an accusation. Wasn't said with malice, but he heard it that way all the same.

"You don't know that."

She raised a brow and shook her head. "Did you?"

She was right. He hadn't. And lunch had gotten lost in the day, too.

He blew out a breath. “Sorry.”

“You need to eat, Apollo. Need to sleep. Need to do something besides sit in front of that computer screen or answer things on this phone.” It wasn’t all that much to ask. He’d taken the time in the past few weeks.

And look how far behind it got me.

No. He was not going to travel that route. Not going to let the worry taint his time with her. “I’m fine.” It was mostly true…if he didn’t think of all the things piling up in the background while he was talking to her.

Kassie shook her head. “I am going to ban that word from our marriage. *We* are never fine. We use the word as a crutch. Right now, you are hungry, exhausted and stressed. You’ve worked nonstop since we got back from the Maldives.” She swallowed. “Don’t make me put on my headset to direct this.”

“Very cute.”

“I know I am.” Kassie shook her hand. “Please give me the phone. Please.”

She shouldn’t have to ask. Shouldn’t have to say the word *please* twice. It was such an easy request. Or it should be.

He should just pass it over. Give it to her and eat. But it vibrated in his hand and he ached to turn it over and look at the text. Just a quick peek.

“Breathe, Apollo.” Her words were soft as she cupped his cheek with her free hand and slid his phone out from him with the other.

His hand was empty. It burned. He wanted it back. Needed it back.

No. I don't.

"Breathe."

He laid his head on top of hers. "I can do this."

"Breathe? I hope so." Kass kissed his collarbone.

Apollo ran a hand along her back. "I meant balance everything." He felt her stiffen in his arms, but she didn't say anything.

"How was your day?" He stepped out of her arms and instantly wanted to step back in. But she was right; he needed food. Particularly because he needed to write at least two thousand words before he hit the sack. Ideally three.

She shrugged. "A day."

He walked to the kitchen and pulled out the cold cuts the chef left in the fridge. It was quick. Filling, and would let him get back to it as soon as he did a short debrief of her day. "What's the meaning of *a day*?"

She hadn't technically said *fine*. But her tone suggested a similar feeling. Once upon a time, he might have let that slide, but not anymore.

He fixed himself a quick plate and grabbed a dessert for himself and her before walking back to the counter where she was already sitting in a high-top chair. "Come on. Out with it."

"It's nothing." She shook her head. "You have enough on your plate. Though I am not sure that you have enough food on your plate."

Kassie hopped off the chair. Her belly was growing but she was still remarkably graceful. She was also ignoring the question.

"Kass, if I want more food, I'll get it." He swiveled the chair and crossed his arms. "I can't eat if I'm worried about you."

"There is nothing to worry over. I just..." She let out a heavy breath. "I think Signa is trying to sideline me. And then I think that is ridiculous. Because of course she isn't. But there are just some indicators. I was so sure I was nearly a shoo-in for partner. Everything went great with my last event. Since I've been back..."

The words died away but she didn't need to say them. He'd only met her boss a handful of times, but Kassie was better than her. When you hired someone better you had two options. Use that skill and make it work perfectly for you, or sideline it until the person quit so you never felt topped.

Unfortunately, most people didn't like being second in their own operation.

"You're a senior planner. The best senior planner." He took the plate of fruit she offered.

"Bias, thy name is Apollo." She winked.

"Damn right, I'm biased. You are the best, Kassie. I am biased but I am also an astute businessman."

"I know." She playfully held up his phone. Now she was trying to distract him. It wasn't going to work.

He grabbed her hand, pulled his phone from it and set it to the side before linking his fingers with hers. "I am serious, Kass. You are the best they have."

"You've only seen me in action on one wedding." She grabbed a piece of fruit and popped it into her mouth.

That was true. But he'd watched her take a wedding scheduled for Stockholm in a few weeks and transfer the whole thing to the Maldives. In less than seventy-two hours. There was no way tons of people could handle that.

"Why do you think you're being sidelined?" She was tired; pregnancy didn't allow the body to rest as easily as people assumed. A multiple pregnancy really didn't allow for good rest. Maybe she was reading too much into things. Though he doubted it.

She picked up an apple slice, paying it far too much attention. "Just little things."

"Like?" He wasn't sure if she didn't want to voice the actions or if she was still trying to fit into a mold that wasn't needed in their home. They were partners. But he couldn't help her if she didn't let him know.

"Missing meetings from my calendar. And Signa put Liza on one of my accounts, as a backup. It's probably nothing, but Liza is the other one up for partner and…"

And while technically, pregnancy was not allowed to factor into hiring practices, it was hard to prove. Particularly if two candidates were both qualified. It was easy enough for the person getting ready to go out on mat leave to find themselves on the *thanks for applying but we went in a different direction* conversation.

"You ever think of running your own business? You would be great." If Signa cut her out, then that was the best solution. He'd done it to a few of his early bosses. Men who hadn't wanted him to outshine them.

Men who'd had to sit on the opposite side of a boardroom table when he was signing the papers acquiring their firms and thanking them for their no-longer-needed services.

"No." The look she shot him was hard to read.

"Why not?" It was the easiest solution. Not having to answer to anyone...except the clients.

He held up a hand. "Running your own business lets you have the final say. The control. The ability to make things happen. Set your own schedule. Do as you please."

"Like you do?"

She had him there.

"I am in control." *Mostly.* "I have the final say." *Usually.* "And I have set my schedule quite well recently." *If one didn't look at the ever-accumulating tasks that are taking over my brain.*

Kassie rolled her eyes. "Come on, Apollo."

"I'm serious, Kassie." And he was.

If her boss was cutting her out, then he could make this happen. Easily. Have a corporation set up or at the very least a limited liability company in her name.

"I know you are. I also know that you are deflecting the conversation we were having about you and what you need to get through the next few nightmare weeks that you have set up for yourself."

"You understand deflection well." He regretted the words as soon as they left his lips. "That was uncalled for."

"It was." She took his empty plate and hopped off the chair again. "It was also the truth. I am quite skilled at it. Learned it at home. Just like you learned setting unachievable goals in your home."

Except I achieved them.

At least he had the foresight not to let those words loose. "Sorry, I just don't want to discuss everything that needs to get done. I will get it done. I will." He'd always found a way.

Not quite. He'd balanced work and left her out. But that wasn't happening now.

He just had to be better. Just a little better. Push a little harder.

"All right. I'm tired and going to bed." She came up beside him and kissed his cheek. "Don't stay up too long."

Don't stay up too long.

Such a simple statement. One that wouldn't mean much…if they weren't the words she'd whispered to him almost every night before she walked out. Not this time, though. This was a short-term thing.

It was.

* * *

Kassie wasn't surprised to roll over and find the bed already empty. His phone had started ringing the second they landed on the runway. A reminder that the three days they'd carved for themselves might be an anomaly. It was frightfully easy for him to slip back into the mold she'd witnessed for so many years.

A mold she feared she was stepping right back into as well.

I said I loved him. He didn't say it back.

She bit the inside of her cheek as she slid off the bed. She'd said it by accident. Slipped past it. But Apollo was so good at calling her out when she tried to slide other things away in their conversations. That, he'd let her push right past.

Not the point. At least not the point right now. She needed to see if he was all right. See if he'd even come to bed.

She doubted it.

Kassie was keeping an eye on the ever-growing lists on the sticky notes covering the corner of his desk. She'd once joked that Apollo could keep an entire printing press in business with the number of stickies he put all over the office.

Since she'd barged into his office, Apollo had been present. Every single day. She'd assumed that meant that he was stepping back. Taking a break.

She should have guessed that what it really meant was he was cramming everything into an incredibly tight hole. Still accomplishing grand things.

Still finding ways to make sure everyone was happy. Everyone had what they needed.

Sure, he worked from home right now. But that didn't mean he was actually taking on less.

He was crashing. Whether he realized it or not. Or rather, whether he wanted to admit it or not.

Stepping up to the door of the office, she could hear him typing. Furiously.

"Apollo?" She knocked then stepped in and tried to keep her expression even. Though it wouldn't matter if horror was etched in her features because he didn't turn around. But the tightness in his shoulders hurt from this distance.

The man needed a vacation. *Another one.*

Who the hell was she kidding? He needed a sabbatical.

"I'm coming to bed soon, Kass. I just need to finish this chapter." The words were breathless. Said as fingers raced over keys and his shoulders tightened even more.

So this was her worst nightmare. "Apollo, it's five in the morning. Did you not sleep at all?" There was no way even his high-functioning brain could produce work at true exhaustion levels.

And that didn't take into account the sheer unhealthiness issues, either.

"Five? No. That can't be right. I just checked the clock." He pulled a hand across his face, typed a few more lines, then turned the chair toward her.

The bags under his eyes and the hollows in his

cheeks showed just how far he was pushing himself. "Guess I lost track of time."

At least there was a little color creeping into his face. Embarrassment was not going to fix exhaustion.

"This isn't losing track of time." She pursed her lips. She didn't want to argue. The solid relationship she'd thought they were building felt a lot more fragile as she looked at the man burning himself out.

He stood and cringed before he started stretching. His body had to ache from sitting in one position for so long.

"Did you fall asleep at your desk?" *Please don't tell me that you've been at this all night.*

Apollo yawned and rolled his head from one side to the other. "I mean, I crashed on my keyboard once, but I don't think it was for that long." He cracked a smile.

A smile!

What the hell was wrong with him!

"I haven't done this in a few years." He stretched his arms in front of himself.

Was there almost a hint of pride?

"You shouldn't be doing it at all." She crossed her arms and looked at the screen where an email notification was going off. It wasn't even six and already emails were pinging in. When was he supposed to just live?

"Eh, every once in a while it's good for the soul to work through the night."

She knew her eyes were huge. Knew her mouth was hanging open. "Which of your parents told you that?"

"Both." He said the word with no heat. No pain. No acknowledgment that it was such a terrible statement. "Father was more succinct. He's quiet. Lets my mother rule, but he wants success as much as anyone. Maybe more."

Except it wasn't his success he was driving. It was his sons'. Success he took credit for but did little to actually achieve besides hurl quieter insults. Success wasn't earned by them!

"My mother was harsher."

Of course she was. It wasn't enough to quietly suggest your son work himself into the grave, so you had something to brag to your society "friends" about. No. Better to make sure he knew his place through fear, screams and threats. So that even when he wasn't in your life he didn't forget it.

He let out another yawn and seemed embarrassed by the wholly normal action. "But I mean, I did it regularly in uni and in the early days of the company."

"You realize that is terrible advice."

"It's not." He bent his head to kiss her cheek but she stepped out of range.

"So you plan to tell our children that this—" she gestured to him and then to the computer "—is a good idea?"

"No. I don't plan to tell them that. But it worked for me."

Did it?

She didn't want to ask that. Didn't want to fight.

Or maybe she just wasn't sure she'd like the answer.

"I have an early meeting but I am going to be home early and we are going to bed at a reasonable hour." She saw him shift. "Is there anything on your plate that I can take?"

She couldn't write mysteries or deal with the business, but she could type up notes. Handle phone calls. Head off calls.

He shook his head.

"Really, Apollo. There has to be something."

"You could book a babymoon."

"I'm serious, Apollo."

He grinned, a little lopsided with exhaustion. "So am I. Book it for—" he pinched his eyes closed "—two weeks. That way we have a guaranteed date for just us. Together. No work. No phone."

"No work and no phone?" It meant the next two weeks would be like hell. "Can you get the book done in that time? With everything else?" She knew the answer. No. But he needed a break.

He shook his head. "The book will be fine. If I have to reach out to my editor to push the date, I will." It looked like it pained him to get the words out. But he said them.

"Actually, that is what I will do. Push the deadline." He straightened his shoulders.

"Are you sure?" He'd never missed a deadline.

He could but she wasn't sure he knew that.

She waited but he didn't say anything. "Apollo? Are you sure?"

"Yep. Book it."

There was a look on his face but maybe it was just exhaustion. "I am holding you to the no phone. No work. Just us." The man was the definition of burning the candle at both ends. There was no place for anything else.

The twins aren't even here yet.

The fear pushed through her mind. This was what he looked like trying to balance everything now. In a few months…a few years…

She swallowed those concerns as they bubbled up her throat. He was too tired to have that conversation right now. But they did need to have the conversation.

"I will book a retreat. Two weeks from now. But you need rest. Now!" She held up a hand, forestalling whatever argument was brewing. "You may have done this is uni but you are not a nineteen-year-old rolling off to your next class. You are thirty-five. A very handsome thirty-five."

"Handsome?" He raised a brow.

She rolled her eyes. "Yes, handsome. But that does not change the fact that you are clearly exhausted. Your clients won't appreciate it. That will put you off even more. So—" she stepped back and pointed to the door "—bed!"

Apollo leaned down, brushed his lips against her cheek and then gave her a playful salute. "A quick power nap probably wouldn't hurt."

A few hours was the bare minimum right now. But it was all he had.

His computer dinged but she grabbed his face before he could look back at it. "Bed!" Then she pushed him out the door. Though realistically, she understood that he had let her win that round. Still, it felt good.

She waited for a moment, but he didn't step back in. Another ding from the computer. How did the man not get annoyed with so many emails and notifications popping in? She headed over to the computer, not quite sure what she was looking for.

She slid into his chair and looked over the last few lines of the manuscript he was so hunched over when she walked in. They were garbled with missing words and misspellings.

Not surprising. When typing at speed the brain tended to get ahead of the fingers, but she was pretty sure most, if not all, of this would need rewriting.

Kassie looked at the wall where he was keeping his timeline. The days slipping further and further away.

Another ding; this time his agent's name caught her eye.

She didn't read the email, but she copied the email address. She wasn't sure why but it felt good to have it.

CHAPTER THIRTEEN

"THE SUNSET IS PERFECTION."

"*You* are perfection, *amore*." Apollo leaned over and kissed her. They'd sat on the beach under the umbrella for the past two days. Perfection didn't begin to describe this time. He'd spent two weeks with his nose to the grindstone. The book wasn't done but he'd come on the trip.

And he'd held to the no-work line…when she was awake.

She pressed her lips to his and stood, her hands pressing on her lower back.

"You all right?" She was heading to bed early each night. Not that he minded. She needed her rest and it gave him a little time to catch up. It wasn't really breaking their pact not to work on the trip since she was already in bed.

He wasn't sure she'd agree. The mental claw squeezed but he pushed the offender away.

Kass looked over her shoulder and playfully rolled her eyes. "I shift for a moment, and you worry something is wrong with the babies."

"You're pregnant with twins, Kassie. I'm just

checking." He stood and looked back at the beach house where they were going to have to visit more often when she wasn't pregnant.

Though with newborns and the winter schedule he had at the office, that was unlikely to happen until at least next summer. But still, he mentally added it to the calendar of things to do he kept running in his mind.

"Just checking." She nodded. "I appreciate that, but I am uncomfortable sometimes." She ran a hand over her expanding belly. "I blame *your* children."

He chuckled and put an arm around her shoulder. "I enjoy how they're mine when they're in trouble."

"Oh." Kassie pulled back. "I didn't mean it that way."

The color drained from her face.

"It's a standard joke, Kassie. Cliché one, even." The look on her face was devastating. There was no reason for her to react to her own statement with such horror. "Seriously, Kass, it's not a big deal."

"Sure. Right. Of course not." The peppy sound was there but there was more to the simple statement.

He turned her in his arms. "Why did the joke bother you? And don't apologize." He'd stopped counting her sorries. She wasn't doing it often; in fact, it was only when she felt terrible about something.

There was no reason for her to feel bad about anything, but the playful joke wasn't so playful now that she wasn't apologizing for just existing.

She pulled her bottom lip through her teeth. "It's nothing. I just…nothing."

"I think it's something." He lifted her chin. "Your dad say that to your mom?"

"No." She laughed. "Are you kidding? My dad barely noticed me and my brother. In fact, I think when Lars cut them out of his life, Dad just shrugged and went on with their lives. He'll inherit the title when Dad passes, but he's more than four-hundred members down in the line of Swedish succession. So it hardly matters."

"We should visit him sometime. I haven't been to New York in forever. He won't set foot in this country again and run even the tiniest risk of seeing our parents." She ran her hand over her ever-expanding belly.

There was a lot to unpack in those statements. None of it related to the question he'd asked. At least not directly.

She was drifting off topic. It was a habit he'd noticed when she didn't want to talk about certain things. She'd wander around the subject. On the edge of it. If he wasn't paying attention, he could miss that she'd never answered the question. It was a tactic he was certain she'd used successfully in their marriage.

It was also a trick that he didn't think she knew she did.

"So your mom said it? Or something similar?"

"I guess." Again the shrug.

"What did she say?" He knew she remembered.

That it was seared into her soul. A prick in her heart that bled even now. Maybe it didn't gush, but a subtle cut that never quite healed.

He had more than a few of his own. He knew the feeling. All too well.

"Apollo."

"Why don't you want to say it?" He knew all the hits from his childhood.

If you just try harder.

Perfection is the only goal.

You don't want to be your brother.

It was that last one that stuck with him. The one that ensured he'd tried harder. Worked harder. Accomplished everything. Never failed…until he almost let her slip through his fingers.

Kassie looked at the setting sun. "My mother didn't want me." She crossed her arms and walked toward the sea. He walked with her.

"She used to say my father wanted two and she got stuck with me." She didn't look at him. He was certain she was seeing something, or someone. Maybe her tiny self, listening to a horrid banter only her mind could replay.

He'd never been fond of his in-laws but he'd been civil. If he'd known…

I should have.

"No matter what I tried, I was never quite right. A little too messy at parties. Too loud. My jokes not the right version of funny. I didn't fit the pretty princess mold I was supposed to. At least not perfectly. And when I messed up, it was something along the lines of *You're the mistake your father demanded. Your father's child.* Those were her favorite phrases. Always together. Always with a sneer." She kicked the water.

Kassie looked at him, tears glistening in her eyes before she turned away. "The worst part is I can't even blame her."

"Like hell you can't." How could she possibly say that?

Kass kicked the water again as she watched the sun giving its last bursts to them. "What I mean is that it isn't fair to blame her."

"Why not?" He was impressed with his soft tone when what he wanted to do was scream the words out. He had more than a few things that he wanted to say to the baroness. More than a few choice phrases that he wanted to make sure were seared into her brain.

But the woman was miles away. And calling her wouldn't be nearly as satisfying.

"Mother wanted more."

She had everything anyone could want. More money than she could spend in a lifetime. What more could she desire?

"Meaning?"

She bent down and picked up a shell, running her thumb over the ridges.

"Did you know that my mother was a painter?"

Was she shifting topics again? "No."

Kassie lifted the shell in her hand, looking at the

sandy object. It held her attention for a few moments before she let the ocean reclaim it.

"She was. My father told her there was room for one job in their marriage. His." She took a deep breath. "She gave up everything for him. I think she lost herself."

Lost herself.

Like Kassie had before she left him.

"That is no excuse for treating you like you weren't wanted." Maybe it wasn't her plan, but Kassandra and her brother were still her children. Still deserved to be seen as more than pawns.

Kassie ran a hand over her belly. "I wasn't wanted. She never lied to me. I knew my place." She looked at him and placed a hand on his cheek.

"*I knew my place?*" Apollo took her hand, pressing his lips to each of her fingers. "That is horrid."

"Maybe. But you're the same."

"I'm not." He dropped her hand, not intentionally, but the words she'd uttered burned.

She looked at him and smiled. "You were raised for perfection by your parents."

"And I fell short. The shine is off the gold there." The words were out, and he wished there was a rewind button. They were supposed to be a joke. Instead, they'd dropped out far too harshly.

"What do you mean?" She tilted her head.

Damn.

He'd helped her shift topics.

"No, Kass. We are talking about you." He put his hand on her belly. "You are perfection. You rule the world in your little headset when you are event planning."

"You and the headset." She winked.

A little color slipped up his neck. "I like the headset. But you know your career matters, right?"

"Sure."

"No, I mean it matters. When the twins are here, you still get to have a career. I mean, maternity leave and all that, but you still get to have both."

"Do I?"

The words were so low that he didn't think she'd meant to say them.

Apollo pulled her to him, kissed the top of her head. "Yes. You do. It's your place. It's so clear when you are there."

"The headset, right?" She let out a little laugh.

"Yeah."

"It's the only place I feel like me." She let out a sigh against his shoulder. "Which means I probably should give you a bit of a pass on always being at the office."

"I don't feel like myself at the office." The words were out. The truth settling around him. No. That wasn't right.

It wasn't the truth. He liked the office.

Maybe *like* was too strong of a word. He was just enjoying being out from behind the CEO desk.

He was the CEO. That was what mattered.

"What about when you're behind the desk writing mysteries?"

"We aren't talking about me." He wasn't letting her shift the conversation. Not again.

She lifted her head, the last pieces of the sunset hitting her brown locks. "We could."

"Not tonight, *amore*." He brushed his lips against hers and lifted her in his arms. He didn't want to discuss why he felt hollow at the company he had built. Why he only felt whole with her and when he was writing mysteries.

Though he was still weeks behind on his story. He'd started an email to his editor, cc-ing his agent to make sure they were in the loop for any possible negotiation that needed to happen. The words left his fingers but as he'd stared at the screen he couldn't force himself to hit Send.

He had time. It would be tight.

Very tight.

But doable. Absolutely doable.

Couldn't let failure happen.

It wasn't failure.

Feels like it.

"We're on vacation, and I want to spend the rest of the night worshipping my gorgeous wife."

"Apollo!" She let out a gasp and immediately threw her arms around his neck. "Before too long, I'll be too big for you to carry me."

"I will always carry you." He kissed her cheek and took them up the stairs.

Kassie looked out the windows of the villa. The sea was lapping on the beach and she let out a soft sigh. It was gorgeous here. This was a reprieve she hadn't known she needed. Which was wild considering that Apollo was the one burning through so many working hours.

All she had to do was put final touches on her last wedding of the season. But everything for that one was running beautifully.

A buzz rang out behind her and she turned but didn't see Apollo. What was that noise? The coffeepot he'd put on a timer as soon as they'd walked into the villa wasn't scheduled to start for another ten minutes.

She'd slipped out of bed while he was still dead to the world. Whoever said you needed to sleep before the baby got here needed a solid slap up the back of their head. Because she was rarely able to sleep past six now. Her bladder was the babies' toy. And she still had almost half of the second and all of the third trimester to go.

The buzz went off again. Where was that coming from?

They'd sworn their cells were off for this vacation. Technically, she'd made him promise not to bring it on vacation but that wasn't really possible in today's modern world. So they'd placed them in the safe the first night. A symbol that work, and everything else, was off the table when they were here.

Just them. The two of them. A holiday extravaganza where nothing mattered but Apollo and Kass.

She'd gone to bed before him last night…and

every night before that. The babies pretty much wanted her in bed by nine and up at five. Their schedule not hers.

The buzz went again, and she slipped her hand between the couch cushions.

The cell was in her fingers and she bit her lip before pulling it out.

They'd promised.

It wasn't a big deal. It wasn't. She'd already gone to bed. It wasn't like he was stealing time from them.

Another buzz.

Who was trying so hard to reach him?

In the event of an actual emergency, the staff had ways of making sure they were informed of everything.

She saw the first message.

Work. Of course.

Thanks for handling that crisis last night. And the night before. I think the Jenkins account is finally settling down.

She swallowed. So this wasn't a one-off note.

I appreciate you answering last night. I got the client under control. Mostly. We need to meet with him when you get back. First thing. H.

Kassie pulled in a breath. So he'd put nothing away for this trip. This was supposed to be a break.

A way to relax from a place that he'd said didn't make him feel whole. A place he'd given so much time to. A place he'd stepped back from, but still brought with him on vacation.

She should put the phone down. But she scrolled through the notifications of a phone that never seemed to quiet.

Deadline looming.

The title of the email caught her off guard. Deadline looming? That couldn't be right. He'd told her he was asking for a push. He'd said it before he left.

The coffee kicked on, and she slid the phone into the pocket of her robe as she heard his feet round the corner.

"Morning, beautiful." He walked over, kissed her cheek then headed to the kitchen and fixed his coffee. "Did you sleep alright?"

"How far did you push your deadline?" The question wasn't planned. Wasn't even a good one. But she needed to know if he'd actually done it. If he'd taken the step for himself. For them. To give him time.

"What?"

"How far did you push it?" She forced her hands into the pockets of the robe. The phone buzzed in her fingers, and she watched his gaze go to the pocket.

"Kass."

"How far, Apollo?"

He pursed his lips. "I started to drift to sleep last

night, and I forgot to put that away. Since you have my phone, I assume you know the answer."

She hadn't snooped. Not really. She'd seen the headers on the notifications. That was all.

"I didn't open the email." She wanted him to tell her that he'd followed through. That he'd given himself some grace. But he'd already confirmed what she suspected.

Apollo looked at her pocket then lifted his gaze to her face. "I can still make the deadline. I'll have to push when I get back. But I can make it. I did a chapter last night."

How late had he been up last night? No wonder he wasn't stirring when she snuck out of bed. He was exhausted. Secretly burning the candle at both ends.

"Why didn't you push it?" He'd sounded sure. At least for Apollo.

"Because I can get it done." The words were so level. So sure. Almost cold. Like he'd separated himself from them.

She looked at her feet and then back at him. "But you don't have to. You could push the deadline. You can take a break."

"I don't *need* a break. I'm fine." He crossed his arms. "I can get it all done. It's not that big of a deal. I'm fine."

Kassie let out a sigh. *I'm fine.* He'd said it twice. Like if he said it enough it might be true.

"Fine. What a word. When women use it, we're accused of hiding behind it. Labeling everything *fine* rather than addressing the problem." She'd hidden behind it so often in their union. Burying her actual feelings. Pretending. Hoping that after a time, it would be true.

"That's not what I am doing." He said the words too fast and she saw the moment it registered.

"You are so important to me." She put her hand in her pocket, her fingers running over the phone. "So important."

I love you.

Her heart screamed the words but her tongue refused to let them slip out. She'd said it once and he'd made no mention of it. She would not say it again. Not first.

She was very aware that he'd started calling her *amore*. Italian for *love*. A nickname but not the actual words. It wasn't the same.

She was *always* reaching out first. She couldn't do it again. She just couldn't.

"You're important to me, too, Kass." The words were soft. Calling directly to her heart.

She believed him. She did.

But she stayed where she was.

"What if you weren't important to anyone else?"

He shook his head. "I'm not."

She knew he misunderstood her. Knew he thought she meant lovers. "You are a CEO. An author. A Nobel winner." His parents had instilled in him that if he didn't have accomplishments, awards, people constantly looking to him, that he wasn't anything.

I was his failure... What if he just wanted me back to fix that black mark?

The thought was so horrid, her stomach turned. But her brain latched on, focused on what she worried might be a truth she hadn't wanted to see.

"Yes. I've accomplished a lot. And there is still a lot of life left. So much to accomplish." He grinned, but there wasn't happiness behind his eyes. Did he realize that?

No. She was sure he didn't.

"I am fine being a nobody."

"You aren't a nobody." The words were harsh. Bitten out as he took a step toward her. "I know your mother—"

"That isn't what I mean. I don't need a legacy, Apollo. I am not trying to earn my place in the universe. I'm happy with the place I have. Are you?"

"Of course." There was a look in his eye. A hint that made her want to believe he meant it.

But the straight line of his lips sent a shiver down her spine.

"If the company failed—"

"It's not going to." Words said too quick. Words spoken in fear.

"I didn't say it was. I said *if*." She stepped toward him. "If it went away, or you stepped down, if you missed your deadline..." She held up a hand to forestall the immediate response she saw building in his features.

"If all that fell away, you'd still be one of the

richest men in Europe. Never have to work a day in your life. If it all fell away."

"It isn't going to fall away. How can you even say that?"

"Because it doesn't make you happy." She took the phone from her pocket and handed it to him. "We promised that this week would be for us. No phones. No work. No outside world. Just us."

"I know." He pushed a hand through his hair. "I know. But you were in bed. I have been present every waking hour. Just us."

That was true. There was no fault in those words. He'd never looked at his phone. If he hadn't foolishly left it in the couch she'd never have known.

Somehow, that made it worse.

"I worry that you don't know what you want."

"I do." He shrugged. "I know what I want, *amore*."

Amore.

There it was again. It was sweet. And so close to *I love you.*

So close.

Kassie looked out at the sea. "We've had four days. Almost a week, if you think about it. We should go home. You need to focus on that book. The deadline will be here before you know it. That way you won't be up all night and burning the candle at both ends."

She turned, hoping he might argue. Say no. That he could just push the deadline now. Make a change.

Apollo nodded. "If you're sure."

Kassie swallowed; she'd made the offer. She couldn't get upset at the response. *Not true.* She could. It just wasn't fair. "Would it help you?"

She watched him hesitate. He didn't want to say yes, even though it was true. "Apollo, would it help?"

"Yes."

"Then I'm sure." She stepped up to him, kissed his cheek. "I'll go pack." But when they got home she was emailing his agent. If he wouldn't take the step, maybe she could at least find out if it was possible? And what, if any, consequences there were. Maybe she could alleviate one of his burdens.

At least a little.

CHAPTER FOURTEEN

I AM GOING with Liza. It's nothing to do with you.

The words were still rattling in Kassie's head after her meeting with Signa that morning. They were sharp edges that coated every thought. She shouldn't have been surprised. In fact, part of her wasn't.

That didn't change the hurt coating the two sentences that ended the dream she'd worked for for two years. Two years building the life she'd created when one dream failed.

A dream that was back on track…at the expense of what she'd worked so hard for.

Two sentences to end it all.

Sure, there were words said after them. A lot of them. All platitudes about how great Kassie was. How she was one of the best.

A carefully worded statement.

One of the best.

Not *the* best.

No way to push back. No way to say there'd been a mistake. No way to redress what she suspected was a decision based purely on the fact that she was pregnant.

There was no way to prove that, of course.

Just a suspicion that would haunt her…maybe forever.

Signa had made her choice.

Liza was her partner.

And my new boss.

Whether that was because Signa wanted to give Liza a senior planner to *mentor* or because Signa didn't want to manage the woman she'd basically said was a shoo-in for the job three and a half months ago.

Three and a half months.

She ran a hand over her belly. The twins were moving, kicking. It was constant.

Five months ago her life was on a different path. She bit her lip as she applied mascara in the small bathroom at the office.

Waterproof.

She'd already cried off the mascara she'd put on this morning.

Her emotions were tight enough to break at a moment's notice. But she was not going to break—again. Not in this office. Not where Signa or Liza could see their fallout.

She made it out to the car, after giving Claire the rest of the day off. Tomorrow she'd pull herself back together. Walk back in with her head held high.

Today was the worst but it was also the best.

They were seeing the twins. An ultrasound that would tell them the sex of their babies. Something she was definitely going to cry for.

She was happy. She'd wanted children. Wanted a life with family.

She'd also wanted that partnership. Wanted to do it all. And a tiny part of her was frustrated at herself.

More than a tiny part.

Her mother had whined about not having her career. About being second to her father. About not getting exactly what she'd expected.

Kassie had promised herself that she wouldn't fall prey to the same feelings. That she'd never want more than her family. Never yearn for something at the expense of her children.

And yet…

She pulled into the parking lot of the women's clinic and frowned. No Porsche sedan. Apollo wasn't here.

Yet.

Yet. Apollo wasn't here yet. He was tapped out at all levels, but he wouldn't miss this appointment. She was just devastated.

But she wasn't telling him about the partnership. Not until after this. She was not stealing the joy of the moment.

"Ms. Nilson. Are you ready to come back?"

She smiled at the receptionist. "Can we wait? My husband is running late."

He hadn't texted her. Hadn't called.

She ran her hand over her phone. This week's worth of texts looked so familiar. Kassie reaching out. One-to-two-word answers coming back. Just like before. Her texting. Him taking forever and giving little to no response.

At the penthouse he was squirreled away in the office. She'd taken him food every night. Except last night. She'd hoped not delivering it would force him out.

He didn't even step out when she said she was going to bed.

The distance she couldn't seem to cross since getting back from the villa was why she hadn't told him that Signa had cut her out of every appointment this week. She'd told him that things were happening. But he hadn't asked for days.

Part of her wanted to believe that she was acting this way to avoid exacerbating his already heavy load.

Once more I'm sliding back into the role I played before.

She mentally cringed. There was nothing wrong with helping him out right now. With prioritizing his needs. She'd tell him tonight or maybe sometime when he wasn't so stressed.

If he didn't have so many things on his plate...

He does and he is still trying to be as present as possible. That has to count for something.

Her brain was in overdrive while her heart kept playing defense.

He was exhausted and yet the man refused to

stop. Refused to put down the mantle his parents had draped over him in the cradle. Perfect Apollo.

She sent a quick text.

Any chance you are on your way?

Another text. Sent by her. Waiting. There were many things unstated right now. So many discussions that needed to happen. Things they were each seemingly holding in.

Sliding back into the habits they'd had. The habits that had destroyed them before.

"Ms. Nilson, have you heard from him?"

She shook her head. "Let me call him." The nurse sent her a sympathetic glance.

Why wasn't he here?

She let the phone ring. When the message took over, she swallowed the bile rising in her throat.

Her phone buzzed and her eyes welled with tears.

On my way where, amore?

Amore.

Another unstated thing. She'd told him she loved him. He never said it. He called her *amore*.

It meant love.

That should be enough.

Should it?

Either way, that didn't matter anymore.

He'd sworn he'd be here for every appointment. That was his solemn vow.

And she'd nearly believed him. Fool me once. Shame on you.

Fool me twice.

"Ms. Nilson. I am sorry but we have a schedule."

"Of course."

"Do you want to reschedule?"

"No. I'm ready." Her heart broke. But she'd gotten through this before. She knew how to do it.

And she wasn't going to make the same mistake twice.

The claw had chased him all day. His brain was mush but he didn't have time to slow down.

Kass had called him while he was finally getting a scene to work. After all this time he knew what he had to do. She'd asked if he was meeting her, but he had no idea where. He'd had his assistant clear his calendar for the day. To sprint to the end of this book.

And she'd not responded to his question. His body was buzzing. The other shoe wasn't going to drop. They were going to make it through everything.

Why do I want to?

He mentally blinked that thought away. She asked that question and he hadn't had a good answer. He'd worked so hard to get her back to put his life back together. Achieve perfection.

Sure, it wasn't quite reality. He was behind on his deadline. He was stumbling at the office. Well, not really stumbling, just not on top of everything like he wanted. Henry was doing fine, but it wasn't the same since he'd pulled back.

Pulled back. The past few weeks it was like he had pulled back at home.

At home.

His eyes cut to the picture of Kassie on his desk. A snap made by the wedding photographer in the Maldives. Kassie with her headphones, directing. Her hand resting on her baby bump. She was what he wanted, but home was where he felt like everything was slipping away the most.

He looked at his phone. Still no response from her. That wasn't like Kass. She always responded quickly.

He mentally tried to picture the last time he'd seen her. This morning? No. She'd just called out that she was heading to work.

Last night?

His blood ran cold.

No. Last night he'd said good-night while sitting in this chair, too.

The last time he'd seen her was yesterday morning. She'd kept a smile painted on throughout breakfast while he was attached to his phone, checking the morning markets.

Painted on.

That was an apt description for the past several days. Everything about her was just a little off. A few hairs outside of the bubbly, in-control wife he'd come to know since she'd barged into his office.

Two nights ago, he'd expected her to argue when

he'd said he needed to work as she told him she was headed to bed. Expected her to say that he needed to come to bed. Needed rest.

And when he'd pointed it out, she'd asked if he wanted her to fight him on it. He didn't.

Maybe I do.

No.

He just wanted everything back the way it was when he felt like he was on top of the world.

He looked at his phone. Still no response.

He called Emilio. "Hey, you cleared my calendar today."

"You asked me to."

Apollo pulled a hand across his face. "I know. I know. Was there a luncheon date with Kass on there?"

"No."

Okay. So it wasn't lunch.

"There was an appointment blocked out. It wasn't listed, just private."

A ringing echoed in his ears. He knew exactly what he'd missed. Damn it.

He looked at the clock. The appointment was over three hours ago.

An appointment less than twenty minutes from their apartment. Where was Kass?

Was something wrong with the babies? With her?

Why hadn't he answered the damn phone when she called?

He called her phone. It went to voice mail. Fair. She had every right to be furious with him.

He dialed her office. Maybe she'd gone back there.

"Hello." Signa answered her phone. Where was Kassie, or at least Claire? Her assistant should have answered the phone.

"Why aren't Claire or Kassandra answering her phone?" He didn't bother to keep his tone polite. This woman was cutting Kass out of things.

"After I told Kassandra that she didn't get the partnership, she gave Claire the rest of the day off while she headed to an appointment."

So she hadn't gone back to the office. Not surprising, given the news Signa had just dropped in his lap.

Why hadn't Kass told him?

Maybe she tried. He hadn't picked up the phone.

Damn it. This was almost as far from perfect husband material as he could get!

His throat tightened and his ears were buzzing.

"Obviously, Kassandra is too good for your place. I appreciate you showing her that. When she purchases your company from you, please remember this moment as the one that cost you everything." He hung up. The woman had hurt Kass and she would pay for it. He would see to it. Luckily, the company registration paperwork was complete. She could start it as soon as she wanted.

Okay. Two problems. One fixed. Now, how was he supposed to fix missing the doctor appointment?

He heard the penthouse door open. Heard her let out an expletive. Time was up. He'd have to wing it.

He stepped out of the office. "I'm sorry—"

She was staring at her phone, color in her cheeks. When she looked up at him, the look of rage in his normally laid-back wife nearly sent him to his knees.

"You created a company. Without telling me." Her eyes widened. "A company." She gripped her phone in one hand and an envelope in the other, her jeweled gaze shooting daggers at him.

This was not where he planned to start the conversation but that was fine.

"Signa is going to rue the day she made that poor decision. You are more than capable of taking over the entire industry." He meant every word.

"So now I have to explain to *my* boss that my ex-husband decided he needed to script my life."

"That isn't fair."

"Isn't it? You purchased an apartment without telling me. Better for the babies."

"I wanted a fresh start for us."

"A fresh start. You bought me a new home without asking me what I wanted."

"You called the other one a tomb." She'd said it to his face. He acknowledged the accuracy. Fixed it.

"I spent my entire childhood being controlled. Not fitting into the mold my parents crafted. And now I don't fit into the mold you want, either. I don't want my own business. I didn't ask for it."

"Maybe I know what you want better than you do." He held up a hand. "That came out wrong." This was when the not sleeping was catching up with him. Words, better words, words that were right, were trapped behind a mental wall. One he could almost feel but couldn't access.

"No. I think you got it right the first time. You think you know better."

He pulled a hand across his face. "Kass, if you didn't like the penthouse I would have found you something else. You have to tell me."

"Except I shouldn't have to." Kass shook her head. No tears. Her face fully set. "Because in most marriages, a partner would talk to the other partner before making a huge decision. But not you. You act. In my best interest. I was your wife. Not a child."

"You are my wife. Stop speaking in the past tense."

She stepped up to him. Pushed the envelope to his chest. He didn't want to take it. But his hand came up automatically.

She stepped back. A chasm splitting between them.

The air in the room was gone. His mind was shutting down. All the effort, everything he'd done and he couldn't think. Couldn't make any words come out.

After a second, Kass nodded and then walked out.

CHAPTER FIFTEEN

SHE WAS GONE.

He had no idea how long he'd stood in the penthouse, their penthouse. The one he'd bought without talking to her.

He'd screwed up. He had no excuse. He'd lost everything.

He opened the envelope. There was a simple note tacked to the sonogram images. *These are your pictures of our girls.*

Your pictures.

Meaning she had her own. Meaning she'd planned to leave before getting home.

His phone buzzed and answered without looking, "Kass!"

"No." His brother's tone was firm. Hard. "But she is at our place. I wanted you to know she was safe."

A weight lifted on his chest. She'd gone to Arthur and Gemma's. She was all right.

Physically.

"Thanks. I'm on my way."

"No." The same tone. "I have given orders that you are not be let up."

"Arthur—"

"Kassandra's orders. I'm just relaying them. She told me I could let you know that she was safe and that she hopes you're able to work on your book tonight."

"Book?" Like he could even think without her here. The fact that she was even considering it showed just how much he'd let her slip into the background.

"I messed up." Those words didn't even begin to cover the monumental screw-up. How had he gotten this so wrong?

How had the life he'd had, the one that had all the pieces in place, finally, fallen about so quickly?

"Yeah. You messed up." No platitudes from Arthur. "The good news is that I screwed up really bad, too. Almost lost Gemma."

"The bad news?" Apollo pushed a hand through his hair.

"You have to decide what matters most to you."

"That's easy." Kassie. "The answer was Kassie." It was always Kassie.

"You say that. But if it was easy, your wife wouldn't be at my apartment." When had his brother become so wise?

"What do I do?" Whatever it was, he'd do it.

Arthur let out a long sigh followed by a heavy pause. "Here's the thing, Apollo. If you have to be told, you aren't really making the change."

The line went dead.

He stared at the phone. During the argument, sixteen emails had flown in.

Apollo started toward the office. Maybe if he answered a few things, worked on the book a little, his mind would clear. The path would part.

Apollo took one step, then another and felt like he was traveling backward. Moving to the past. This was what he'd done the first time she'd left. He'd put his head down. Accepted that she was gone even though she'd never signed the papers. She'd gone and he'd felt hollow. But he hadn't gone to her. Hadn't fixed everything. He'd pressed ahead.

Only two tiny miracles had brought her back into his life. A life that was whole when Kassie was in it. A life that offered so much joy…but no awards.

He halted.

She'd told him when she'd barged into his office that she didn't think he could be a husband or father because there were no accolades. He'd mentally challenged that. Focused on being the best husband and father.

Best.

Not present for her and him. Not a loving partner. The best. Like somehow that tag made everything worth it. His parents had cut him off. Marked him a failure.

And rather than look at that for what it was—cruel—he'd marched ahead. Not because he thought it would bring them back into their good graces.

But because he didn't know how to do something if he wasn't winning.

That mindset had cost him the woman he loved. The woman who should never doubt that he'd be there. The woman who'd accused him of controlling her life.

And she wasn't wrong. He knew she'd make a perfect business owner. She had more than all the qualifications. But he'd never asked her. Never checked in. He'd stolen that choice.

And what did he want?

This was what Kass had asked him. What she pressured him to look at in his life.

I want it all.

But look where that mindset had gotten him. He took a deep breath, still stuck between the office and any other room in the penthouse.

Do I want it all?

Or was that something that was drilled into him from birth? That if he didn't have it all, if he didn't do everything right, wasn't the best at every single thing, that he was worthless.

It was such an easy answer. One that nearly sent him to his knees.

He'd wanted the company. But building it was what was fun. Running it every day was bringing him nothing but stress. And the books.

Those he loved.

But he'd never been able to fully give himself to them.

His phone rang. He knew it wasn't her, but he answered it out of habit.

His agent offered a quick hello then started in on the book. Apollo had always appreciated the man's no-nonsense approach. "I saw your wife's email about the extension."

"Extension?" It felt like the universe was dropping the answer into his lap. An answer his wife had helped cement. "She asked you for an extension? For me?" Part of him wanted to be angry. Hadn't she just accused him of doing the same? But another part, the rational part, breathed a sigh of relief. She'd taken a step he could never have taken himself.

"No. She actually asked what the consequences were of such a thing. Said you were super-stressed and she didn't know if it was real stress or something she could help you manage." His agent chuckled.

"That sounds like her." So she hadn't taken away his choice. She'd reached out to find out what his options were.

"Anyway, I already reached out to the publisher. We've pushed a year. Before you start saying you can do it sooner, my wife is getting ready to go out on mat leave. The book isn't up for preorder yet. So, this just makes the most sense. You've never requested a push, and your sales are more than excellent. Given the extra time, maybe you can even fit in the book tour we've attempted to schedule three times."

Book tour. He wanted that. Wanted it badly. This was the answer. The answer he should have easily seen. And wouldn't have without her.

"I love the idea of a book tour, but not this round. My wife and I are also expecting."

"Oh. Congrats, and you should have let me know. I would have requested another year."

"I don't need it. But I appreciate the breathing space. It's perfect."

His agent offered a quick goodbye and popped off the phone. Leaving him with a new direction. Less stress. All because Kass had asked a question for him.

Kass…

He closed his eyes. He loved her. He loved her with every fiber of his being.

Did I tell her that?

Another easy to answer question.

He'd called her *amore*, but never said the words.

Why?

Because he'd worried that she'd said the words first…in the past tense. Rather than tell her he loved her, risk it, he'd waited for her. Wanting her to say it first.

It was always Kassie doing things first. The first to text. The first to apologize. The first to walk away.

Because she couldn't fit into a mold she thought he wanted.

What the hell had he done? She stood by every dream. Even ones she'd pointed out weren't dreams.

And when she'd asked him to do one thing, not to make promises he couldn't keep, he'd blithely told her he'd be at every appointment. Every step. And when his world got busy, he'd let her slip into the background again.

A place she should never be.

If he wanted her, wanted a life with her, something had to give.

No.

Several things had to give.

And it was shocking how easy it was to see the path before him.

Kassie walked into her office and looked at her desk. Twelve hours since she'd walked out of the apartment. Twelve hours since she'd changed her life.

Blown it up, some might argue.

She'd cried herself to sleep last night. Gemma had suggested she take a day off. But what was the purpose?

Besides, Apollo had quit her job for her. It had taken her almost an hour to get Signa to answer the phone. And a thirty-minute discussion with her boss to understand that Apollo didn't speak for her.

She was tired. But she was going to be tired. She was going to be sad. She was going to be alone.

Tomorrow that truth wouldn't be any different.

Tomorrow her heart would still be broken.

The least she could do was continue with the one thing that brought her some joy.

"Morning." Liza walked in with a stack of paper.

"Morning." Kassie looked at the paper, confused. Almost everything in the office was done digitally. Even contracts were signed digitally these days.

"I have a list of notes for the Linberg-Olssen wedding."

A list of notes?

"The wedding's in two weeks, Liza. And moving on perfectly." It was basically the smoothest event she'd ever run. She couldn't say that, though, because she was taking no risks at jinxing it.

"Yes. I know. And there are several things that need doing if we're going to do this right." Liza dropped the papers on her desk, a fake smile plastered on her lips.

"Such as?"

"There are no flowers. I've already spoken to a florist. It will cost us double their rate, but they agreed to get flowers. I texted the bride to get her thoughts on the available flowers."

"The bride doesn't want flowers." Kassie was too tired for this today. What was this weird power play?

"Every bride wants flowers." Liza walked over to Kassie's desk and picked up her phone without asking. "Signa, can you please join us?" She flashed Kassie a smile that held no warmth.

That escalated fast.

"Liza—"

"We'll wait for Signa. I want this on the record."

On the record.

If that was what Liza wanted, fine.

"You two aren't getting along? Already." Signa was exasperated. Before even hearing anything.

"There are no flowers for the Linberg-Olssen wedding. The oversight—"

"There is no oversight. Liza is simply pushing for something because it's my client." That wasn't as diplomatic as it should have been. But she was too tired and broken to play whatever game was happening here.

"Kassandra." Signa crossed her arms. "I expected you to be better after you begged for your job back."

Her mouth was open. She knew that. And she hadn't begged. Not really. Just tried to explain that Apollo hadn't spoken for her.

"I know you are upset about the partnership but to take it out on your new boss and to argue about flowers. What bride doesn't want flowers at their wedding?"

"One whose soon-to-be stepdaughter is highly allergic to all sorts of pollen." Kassie let out a sigh.

"There are flowers without high pollen counts. Roses, hydrangeas."

Claire buzzed in. "I have Dahlia on line one. She isn't pleased."

"I'll handle it."

Before she could lift the phone, Liza pushed the speakerphone option. "Ms. Linberg, this is Liza, one of the partners here. I am so sorry that you were not given the option for flowers. I know how important—"

"Options!" Dahlia's shout rang out in the room. "I told Kassandra no flowers."

Liza's and Signa's eyes widened.

Liza regained her composure. "Did you? Every bride wants flowers."

Wow. If there was a list of wrong things to say, that might be at the top. And this was who Signa had chosen over her.

"I do know that your stepdaughter is allergic to pollen but there are some lovely flowers without high pollen counts so you can still have the option." Why was Liza pushing this so much?

And why was Signa allowing it?

Kassie took a deep breath. "Her stepdaughter panics at flowers. She had a super-bad attack about a year ago. She's only seven. For her to enjoy the day, the bride and groom requested no real flowers. So I worked around that. There will be flowers, paper flowers. I ordered them weeks ago."

She said the words evenly, her gaze never leaving Signa's. At least the woman looked mortified by today's events. "Everything will be fine, Dahlia. No pollen. I promise."

She saw Liza flinch and Signa pursed her lips.

"If I see whoever the hell this Liza is around my wedding, I will make sure no one in my circle uses this planning service again." Then she hung up.

Quite the threat. Dahlia had power in society. A lot of it.

Kassie crossed her arms, not bothering to look at Liza or Signa. "Is this really about flowers? I've never taken on a client and not given them exactly what they want."

Liza let out a huff. "There are still some changes that need—"

"No. The bride and groom signed it off." She looked at Signa. How long was she going to let this go on?

"The wedding is already done, Liza. You'll have more control on the next one."

The words were a slap. More control. She was a senior planner. She handled everything.

Apollo was right. He'd seen what she refused to acknowledge. She wasn't in control here. Not really. And the little she'd had was going to be ripped from her. She could see Liza already plotting to sideline her.

And Signa would just let it happen.

She could run circles around them.

She ran a hand over her belly. Her twins were girls, and she'd make sure to tell them never to let someone treat them this way. So why was she willing to accept less than she was worth for herself?

There is a company.

Apollo's words rang in her ears. It wasn't how he should have handled the conversation. And he should have checked with her first.

He did. I told him no.

The thought was a mental slap. He'd brought up

her own place. Her own company and she'd pushed the idea away.

He'd gone about it the wrong way. The absolute worst way. But Apollo was right. She deserved her own company. A place where she called every shot.

Kassie could see it in her mind's eye. The shop. The planning area. It was like the dream was just waiting for her to take the risk.

A risk her husband had known she needed.

Because of his decision, she was better positioned for what she was about to do. He'd given her a gift she hadn't wanted.

But a gift she needed.

"You're right. In fact, you will have all the control. Consider this my notice. I will stay on until the Linberg-Olssen wedding concludes—only because Dahlia deserves better than to have me leave on her."

Signa's pursed lips nearly disappeared but she didn't argue. That cemented the decision.

"You were probably not coming back once the twins were born anyway." Liza's words were harsh but the look she shot Signa confirmed what she'd never be able to prove. She'd lost the promotion due to the pregnancy.

And just like her mother, she was furious. Unlike her mother, it had nothing to do with the children she loved. She could have a career and her family. It might look different than she had planned but that was life.

She was more than capable of handling everything thrown at her.

"And I am taking the day off." Maybe this wasn't her finest moment, but she needed out of here.

She grabbed her purse and wasn't surprised when Signa didn't try to stop her.

Stepping into the parking lot, she took a deep breath then caught sight of the Bugatti. Sitting in exactly the same place it was months ago.

Her heart tore. She'd made a lot of choices in the past few minutes. She knew what she wanted. Kassie wanted Apollo in her life. But if he needed everything, then they were going to be in each other's lives as friends and coparents. It hurt, but she had to do what was best for her.

"Kass." He leaned against the hood of the car, almost like he'd stepped out of a car ad.

"Apollo." He didn't look like he'd gotten any sleep. But that wasn't a change since the last time she'd seen him.

"I love you." The words she'd longed to hear fell from his lips.

"I love you, too." She wiped a tear away. She loved him. Loved him so much. She wanted to believe it was enough but she wasn't going to fit into anyone else's mold. Not again. "But I can't be perfect, Apollo. I am not even willing to try. I am myself and that is all I am willing to be. No legacy. No reaching for stars. I have dreams but I won't let anyone else's definition of success define me. I get to define me."

"Good."

The word was solid. A true statement. She bit her lip and pressed on. "I love you, Apollo. I love you so much. I never stopped, but I can't sit in the background. I can't take the backseat in your life. I love you and it isn't fair to me. It also isn't fair of me to force you to be someone you're not."

Those were the words she should have said last night. The ones that highlighted how much she cared for him. But also put the boundary in place for what she needed. Words said out of love, even if it acknowledged that love wasn't always enough.

Apollo let out a breath. "I can't lose you, Kass. There is no excuse for missing the appointment yesterday. None. I will never get that moment back."

He crossed his arms, uncrossed them, then redid the motion. "And I hate that it took that happening to wake me up. It should have been when I came home years ago and found you gone. That should have been my crisis moment. And I can't change that it wasn't."

The words were pouring out of him. Was she dreaming or was he actually saying what she needed to hear?

"I stepped down last night. From the company. Still on the board, but I can breathe."

"Wow." The word was soft and all she could force out.

"It's not for you. I mean, it is in a way. But it's really for me. It's what I need." He swallowed and took a step toward her. "I want to write. That's where my heart is, and I don't have to run the company. I can step away."

"You can." She nodded. "The book is still due."

"Yes. But because my lovely wife asked what happened if I asked for an extension, he just did it for me. A year. I have a year. Which I don't need so I plan to take a very extended paternity leave."

So much to process.

"Wow."

"You already said that." He took another step toward her. "The only perfect thing I want in this world is our family and it is perfect simply because it is us."

"Perfect?"

"Yep." He raised a hand and cupped her cheek. "Perfectly messy. Perfectly fun. Perfectly loving. Imperfectly perfect."

She let out a laugh. "Imperfectly perfect. That is nonsense, and I love it."

He bent his head, but she held up a hand. He'd made a lot of changes in the past twelve hours. She'd made a major one, too. And she wanted it in the open now.

"I might need that company you set up."

He raised a brow. "Might?"

She looked over her shoulder at the office that was already no longer hers. Not really. "I officially quit. I mean, I have one more wedding but yeah, umm… I quit."

He pulled her toward him. "I'm proud of you. And I would love to bury this place."

She put her hands on either side of his face. "I don't need that. I just need a career I want. They can have this."

He playfully rolled his eyes. "Fine. But you change your mind, you let me know."

"Deal." She wasn't going to, but it was amazing having him in her corner. Fully. "I love you."

"I love you, too." He dropped his head, capturing her lips.

Time stood still.

When it finally started again, he laid his head against hers. "Any chance I can convince you to come home? We can start looking for a new place. Together."

Together. Was there a more perfect word? "I don't need a new place. You should have asked but I like the penthouse. Love the view. Our girls will be very happy there. So yes, I will come home. But the first thing we are doing is taking a nap."

His lips brushed hers. "*Amore*, it's like you read my mind."

EPILOGUE

THE SUNRISE AT the villa was her second favorite place in the world. The first was anywhere with her husband and the twins.

As if spawned by her thoughts, Apollo wrapped his arms around her and kissed her neck. "Good morning, *amore*."

"Morning." She leaned her head back against his shoulder.

"Enjoying a few quiet moments?" He squeezed her and looked out at the sunrise.

"Yes." She took a deep breath. "I love them, but once the twins are awake, quiet isn't something we know until they're down for a nap."

"And even that doesn't last for long anymore." Apollo chuckled.

At three, their daughters, Aurora and Selene, were still napping but for shorter and shorter durations.

Apollo was still on the board at his company, but his life now revolved around them and his books.

Kassie had expanded her business for the third time last year. She only took on a handful of clients each year, so she got to control her schedule, but she was guiding and mentoring new planners. Claire, now a senior planner, was going to make partner soon, through Kassie's mentorship. The full circle moment was something she never would have had without the man standing behind her.

"Think we can convince them to watch a new show today? I quoted their current favorite in my dreams last night."

They were home with their family. Eating dinner, playing make-believe and watching the same cartoon movies over and over again with their girls.

"Probably not." She turned in his arms. "Pretty boring life. Would you have it any other way?"

Apollo tilted his head and brushed his lips against hers. "Not boring at all. Imperfectly perfect. And I'd have it no other way."

* * * * *

If you missed the previous story in the Billion-Dollar Brothers duet, then check out

The CEO's Perfect Match

And if you enjoyed this story, check out these other great reads from Juliette Hyland

Falling for His Fake Date
Beauty and the Brooding CEO
How to Tame a King

All available now!